TILL THE FAT LADY SINGS

By the same author

Matthew
The story of a faith that survives death

Matthew was a bright ten-year-old having the best holiday of his life with his family in Austria – when he fell and was killed.

Writing as Matthew's father and also as a minister, Bob Jackson tells how the family responded to the tragedy.

Bob Jackson is at present vicar of St Mary's, Scarborough.

TILL THE FAT LADY SINGS

by

Bob Jackson

GODALMING
SURREY

First published in 1996 by Highland Books, Two High Pines, Knoll Road, Godalming, Surrey, GU7 2EP.

Drawings and Cover Picture by Taffy.

British Library Cataloguing-in-Publication Data. A catalogue record for this book is available from the British Library.

ISBN: 1 897913 29 X
Printed in Great Britain by Caledonian International Book Manufacturing Limited, Glasgow.

Dedication

Jesus said,
"I am the resurrection and the life"

To Helensfield Doctor Doolittle who, in the finiest traditions of his breed, did little all his life except be a faithful and willing victim of His Master's Jokes. Heaven will include Retrievers.

Truth is funnier than fiction. Though the characters in this book are fiction, most of the stories are true. I hope they also convey truth about death and new life. Halfway through chapter one, Ammy the steam-age Amstrad gave up the ghost. He was declared dead on arrival at the menders: "Here is your heap of scrap back, sir." Unable to afford a new one, and with a deadline to meet, your author plugged him in for the last time before the great computer dustbin in the sky, laid hands and prayed for healing. He worked perfectly for months afterwards. So I dedicate this book to the resurrection life of Ammy, without whom this tale would not have been written.

Chapter 1

◆

"Morning Vicar," shouted Mabel from the pavement as her vicar unlocked the vicarage car in the vicarage drive and said goodbye to the vicarage wife and the vicarage dog.

"Morning Mabel."

"Morning Vicar," waved Fred Williamson at the vicar's visage in the vicar's car at the traffic lights by the vicar's church.

"Morning Fred."

The vicar drove on. He recalled the supermarket checkout girl last night who had looked startled at the toilet rolls and blurted out in her dumb blonde voice, "Ooh I didn't think vicars needed these."

Breakfast and flatulence churned within. His indigestion started to do his thinking for him.

Lord, why do they call me vicar? mulled the vicar morosely. *Do they think I was never christened? They think I was born with a dog collar.* He fantasised...

> "What is it?" whispers the anxious and exhausted mum.
>
> "Oh look, it's a vicar" replies the midwife as the dog collar uncurls from the umbilical cord.
>
> No-one says, "Morning Solicitor, afternoon Accountant, evening Greengrocer". So why "Morning vicar"? I can hardly remember by own name. "Hello I'm George, who are you?" "Pleased to meet you — I'm er, Vicar."

The vicar shuddered and the vicar arrived. As he locked his car, Mrs Gardener the florist was just leaving.

"It's very windy, Vicar," she gushed.

"And getting worse Flower Power," grumped the vicar as he stumped with griping tum up the path to the tasteful building with the discreet chimney and the tell tale curl of pungent smoke.

With a swift "Morning Superintendent," the vicar headed efficiently for the centre of three doors. The door on the right was labelled 'Gentlemen' and on the left 'Ladies'. He barged without ceremony into the door of his destiny, the central sanctum, the middle cross of Golgotha, the door marked 'Clergy'.

"Lavatorial novelties for the middle sex," he muttered too loudly for his professional decorum. From the small but suitable changing room he could see right into a perfectly normal toilet cubicle, where a perfectly normal man wearing a perfectly normal full length black dress was performing perfectly normally, while maintaining a miraculously bone dry cassock.

"Morning Father," said the vicar.

"Morning Vince," grinned Father O'Brien, and Vince nearly hugged him.

Indigestion and grief have much the same effect on facial expression, so Vincent conducted the first part of the funeral in the chapel with an appearance of immaculate empathy. Feeling uplifted by his appropriate address, Vince sat in the front of the hearse for the short ride to the graveside. The mourners gathered round the grave. Vince struggled to operate the door handle and something snapped inside it. He struggled some more. The door remained solidly locked. Some fringe mourners, noticing his so far secret struggle to join them, began to giggle. Something snapped inside Vincent. A deep anger at the conspiracy of all material things against his ordered life set the cement of his emotions into the concrete of a face designed to hold its battered dignity till the sun froze.

Thus immobilised, Vincent awaited the undertakers' realisation of his absence from the outdoor scene. This took a surprisingly, and to Vince, insultingly, long time. At length, the most mechanically minded of the po-faced bearers forced open the door and Vince emerged with stiff dignity into the gale.

The cloudburst began as the coffin was being lowered. But the Rev. Vincent Popplethwaite, railing against the devilish conspiracy of life's petty elements against all purveyors of the love of Christ, flung the committal words back into the wind and rain. The tears of the mourners mingled with the downpour as his flatulence threatened to meet the gale. Just as he reached the final words "And now unto him who is able to keep us from falling", a great gust of wind whipped his stole from round his neck and flung it into the grave. Leaning forward in horror to watch its descent, Vincent slipped on the soaking soil. The next gust got under his surplice, converting it into a temporary mainsail. In a trice, Vince followed his stole and, in what moderate clergy would call an excess of empathy, landed with a clatter on the coffin lid.

It took all four bearers to haul Vincent out, and a stiff drop of Irish from Father O'Brien's hip-flask to restore him to driving condition.

"Good funeral, dear?" enquired the vicarage wife as her mud encased vicarman squelched through the vicarage hall on the way to the vicarage bath.

"Ruined by wind. I've had the new worst moment of my life," grunted a defeated Vincent as he dragged himself up the stairs.

The smell of 'Fairdoos' coffee wafted up to the bathroom as Vince felt his bruises. It was merely moderately mouth-watering because Vincent only drank it under duress. Janet — his wife — sold it at the 'Fairtrade' stall at church because it helped the Third World and set a good example. She drank it serenely and was totally convincing in her affection for the soil brown brew. She was as saintly about her coffee as she was about most things. This was why Vincent loved her deeply, but also why he found her hard to live with.

"Is there any proper coffee?" he shouted down, full of First World consumer-sin.

"It's the new 'Fairdoos' decaff," was the only reply.

Vince dropped deeper in the bathwater, deliberating a secret trip to the supermarket in the next town, where he wouldn't be recognised, to lay in supplies of the exploiters' decadent and definitely delicious un-decaff.

As he lay there, a new and far more thrilling aroma assailed his nostrils. Bacon. His saintly love was making a bacon sandwich for her battered hero. His heart sang. Time was, when they were young and happy, Janet would skip around the kitchen making his favourite bacon sandwich for lunch while doing three other chores at the same time. But now the crippling pains of arthritis made each movement an effort. The saint below was making the much muddier saint above happy through an act of painful self-sacrifice. The plug was pulled, a fresh dog collar inserted round the clean clerical neck, a tear of pride at his wife's courage shed on the clean clerical cheek, and a restored Vicar of Yawtown tenderly kissed his beloved as he received the treasured double-smoked from her once beautiful but now hideous hand.

Between mouthfuls, Vincent explained what had happened in his dreadful morning and nearly drowned in self-pity. Janet laughed like a drain. Not polite, sympathetic laughter, but gut laughter from way down in the solar plexus. She recovered just enough to blurt out, "And now unto him who is able to keep us from falling...!" before she was at it again. Vincent couldn't see it. All he could see were the bruises appearing all over. He needed a shoulder to cry on, not a helpless heap of hilarity.

Janet stopped herself with a superhuman effort of will.

"I'm sorry my precious, it must have been terrible for you, but it's the best laugh I've had for weeks. I don't find my own aches and pains as funny as yours. What did Father O'Brien say?"

"When you really get your wings, make sure you fly up not down – the accommodation's better!" replied Vincent glumly, and Janet started up all over again.

Vincent sat on the settee, stiff and arms crossed. He couldn't help himself. Despite the bacon, he had taken offence at the only person in the whole wide world who ministered to his needs instead of expecting him to minister to theirs.

"Why?" he railed, "Why does it all go wrong? When we started out, we thought we would change the world, or at least one parish in it. We thought we would fill the church. I thought everyone would love me, and that God would get nearer and nearer and grow bigger and bigger. Instead, I'm in a spiritual desert, I've forgotten how to pray, I don't know how to enjoy myself anymore, St Agatha's still as dead as a dodo, the churchwarden's trying to destroy me, I spend my life trapped in limos and falling in graves, and you're in this state. Why, for God's sake? It's not fair and I've had enough of it."

"Neither was calvary," replied the saint quietly (Vincent looked confused) "– fair," she added patiently, "And Jesus died screaming, 'My God my God, Why?' so I don't suppose being his disciple was meant to be easy. I don't know 'Why?' but we've got to keep the faith Vinney, it's all we've got. And maybe God's got something good for us yet. You've got ten good years of ministry left in you yet, and it's never over till the fat lady sings."

Vincent looked confused and said, "What isn't?"

"Church, silly," murmured Janet, as she stretched to give him a gentle kiss. As lip was about to touch lip, the phone rang. Vincent grimaced, and answered.

"Hello, it's Lee here," said a cheerful voice on the other end. "I'm just ringing to say I've moved in today and the house is a shambles. But it won't matter because the retreat starts tomorrow and I'll have plenty of time to sort it out after the ordination."

"I got ordained thirty years ago, and I still haven't had time to write round the relatives and tell them," responded Vincent. "But I'm looking forward to Sunday — I'll see you at the cathedral."

"Yes, so am I. I've never been in a cathedral before," responded Lee, brightly. Vincent couldn't think of a reply to that revelation, so he grunted and hung up.

"Things should be much better with a curate. He'll take a lot of work off your shoulders if you let him you know," encouraged Janet.

"And a lot of years off my life," muttered Vincent grimly.

Sunday came and the cathedral was packed. St Agatha's had turned out in force for the ordination of the Rev. Lee Green, and seven other churches had done the same for their new curates.

The great organ played impressively, and a huge procession snaked from the side chapels to the back of the nave and then down the centre ailse towards the altar. Choirs, canons, crucifers and clergy converged on the chancel in solemn array. Then came the eight curates to be, magnificent in new robes and dog collars, processing in single solemn file.

The leading nearly-cleric was intending to be a high churchman and had made a fine study at college of all the right rituals. At first he concentrated on holding his hands together in front of him in just the right 'Uriah Heep caught at the very start of a major hand wringing session' way. Then, at precisely the right distance from the chancel steps, he suddenly halted to execute a perfect bow towards the altar. His knees bent and his head went down in the impressively athletic genuflection he had been perfecting for months.

The second in line nearly-cleric was Lee Green. As the great procession wound round the ancient cathedral, Lee, hands swinging by his side, looked up and around in delight. He loved the vaulted ceiling and the giant organ loft, and spotted his mum in the crowd and waved to her. He wasn't really sure what to do, but the guy in front looked like he did, and Lee followed him as closely as he could. But suddenly, as Lee glanced up at a clerestory window, the guy in front stopped and made a back like a vaulting horse. Lee walked into him at full pace, was flung up in the air and catapulated clean over his colleague to land in a heap on the floor in front of him.

As he picked himself up, Lee noticed that the congregation around them all seemed to be in some sort of distress, holding handkerchiefs over their faces and spluttering into them. *A lot of hay fever about at this time of year*, thought Lee as the procession started moving again. The Bishop seemed to be having a problem as well, getting a fit of giggles every time he tried to start the service. *Has he been at the communion wine?* wondered Lee.

Afterwards, over refreshments, Cuthbert Grimshaw, the domineering churchwarden, took Lee on one side to let him know who was boss.

"I've been churchwarden of St Agatha's since before you was born, son," he said, in a gruff, no-nonsense, 'I speak my mind', northern voice. "And when our present vicar arrived four year ago I told him, 'You'll be alright with us as long as you don't try to change anything. I'll oppose any change you suggest, and the church council usually follow me.' And the same goes for you, Reverend Green, you'll be alright with us as long as you keep our traditions. I hope you don't make people shake hands in 'the peace' like the vicar does. We don't come to church to be friendly at St Agatha's — we like reverence Reverend."

As Cuthbert wandered off to find his next victim, another middle-aged man grasped Lee's hand.

"Welcome Lee, I'm Frank Williamson, junior churchwarden. I'd just like you to know we're not all like Mr Grimshaw, and I hope you'll be very happy changing things while you're here." Frank grinned and moved on.

"The warden's a bit creepy, Vince," said Lee as they wandered back to the car park together.

"Yes, Grimshaw by name and 'grim sure' by nature," muttered Vincent darkly. "Ever since I started sharing 'the peace' he's been at my throat. Church council meetings are a monthly nightmare. There's a Cuthbert faction who oppose everything. It's so nasty I could vomit some months. The nice, quiet members have left and he rules the roost. Sometimes I think Old Nick himself controls Cuthbert's larynx and sculpts his scowl. Welcome to the Church of England."

Chapter 2

◆

"Could we try a healing service, Vince?" asked Lee at their first staff meeting. Vince quivered in alarm.

"I don't think we can have faith healing and people leaping up out their wheelchairs here, Lee." But Lee persisted.

"All I meant was that we ask anyone who wants to be prayed with to stay behind, kneeling at the communion rail after they've received communion at the evening service. We used to do that at my placement church at college and I got quite a dab hand at the healing bit."

Vincent remembered that Cuthbert would be on holiday shortly and gave in against his instincts. "OK, two weeks on Sunday evening, and we'll see what happens."

Vincent had advertised the healing service the Sunday before, when Cuthbert was safely in Corfu, and was astonished to see several solid citizens kneeling at the rail to be prayed for. Lee and Vincent both prayed for Frank Williamson's bad back. After the service, Frank bounced up to Vincent and said, "It's gone Vicar, I've had two years of torment with this back and it's better, it's wonderful, God's not a bad bloke, after all, is he?" Vincent was amazed, and quite forgot to be pleased. But he did wonder for the first time whether Lee might actually have something to offer the church as well as being a pain in the neck.

"I've noticed," said Lee, after everyone had gone, "That a lot of them look up at that cross high above the chancel steps when you preach. They seem to venerate it."

"Yes," confirmed Vincent, "The 'Cuthbert Crowd' dote on it. It was donated by one of Cuthbert's ancestors. They seem to gaze at it and draw something from it while I preach. I think they use it to block me out, or to block God out."

"Get rid of it," urged the wild young curate, I bet it's the source of your problem."

"You can't get rid of things in churches, Lee, it's against the rules. I think we're stuck with it," counselled his battle weary vicar.

The next day, Vincent perched himself precariously on the church stepladder and took his first close look at the cross. It was decorated with some pock-marked and particularly hideous figures. In the centre was a soldier holding a three-pronged fork and with horns growing through his helmet. It was like a scene out of hell. Vincent wondered what manner of crafstman had fashioned this thing that had stared down at the congregation for the last century.

An ashen-faced Vincent reported his findings to Janet and lamented his impotence to do anything about it.

"If it's an evil force, pray against it," urged the infuriatingly righteous saint. That evening, the saint started to pray, and even persuaded her husband to pray with her for a while. However, eventually he left her to it and slipped off to bed with a whisky.

Next Sunday, Vincent was greeted at the church door by Arnold, the sacristan. "Have you seen the cross, Vicar? It's got a stress fracture. I went up to clean it first thing, and noticed it. I didn't dare touch it."

Trembling, Vincent tottered up the ladder to take a close look for himself. As he stared at the cross, the centre scene with the demon figure ripped from the rest of the cross with a loud crack and fell resoundingly on to the stone floor below. Vincent wobbled down, shaking, not knowing whether to be overawed, filled with dread, overjoyed, or just confused.

At the church council meeting, Vincent proposed doing away with the old cross and buying a new one. Cuthbert wanted it mended with the fallen pieces put back in place.

"That cross is the heart of St Agatha's and it moves over my dead body."

The PCC voted by thirteen votes to nine to have it repaired, and Vincent slumped home, yet again a defeated man. Janet was already asleep, and Vincent tossed and turned beside her all night.

"Then we'll have to pray again," said Janet over breakfast, as Vincent told her the news. "We'll pray over morning coffee."

At coffee time, Vincent wandered out of the study, having made slender progress with his sermon, was given a mug of steaming 'Fairdoos', and made to sit with Janet on the settee. She got as far as, "Dear Lord, you know the situation and we look to you to sort it out for us." Then the moment was torn asunder by the shrill call of the master, 'he who must be obeyed', the dread din of the tyrant telephone.

"I thought you ought to know," said the voice of Lee on the other end, "it's Cuthbert Grimshaw."

Wearily, Vincent asked, "What's Cuthbert done now?"

Lee, responding with greater gravity than Vincent had thought him capable of, replied, "Consumed his customary cornflakes and collapsed over the kippers. He was dead on arrival at Eastern General."

Vincent's face twisted in an essay, even a thesis, of emotions. Proper and vicarial shock furrowed the same brow that leapt with nervous elation. Lips that quivered with excitement in all four directions at once, still managed with perfect inflexion the proper response, "Oh no, poor Daisy, she depended on him." Daisy was Cuthbert's wife, as blameless as she was clueless.

"I'm off to see her now," said Lee, "I think you'll need a little help with this one after the way he's treated you."

For a moment Vincent appeared to have shut off from the world. Something appeared to trouble him.

"Are you sure he's actually dead? " he quizzed.

"As a Dodo. I was visiting the hospital myself when they brought him in."

"Thanks Lee. Tell Daisy I'll see her soon. I'll phone Frank first." As the receiver was replaced, Janet called from the settee, "What's happened dear?"

"The fat lady just sang for Cuthbert Grimshaw," he replied.

"Phone the hospital and make sure," came the instant, businesslike response. Vincent duly rang and received the clinical confirmation.

"Well, I'm very sorry dear, you know I've always prayed for that man, but it'll unlock all sorts of doors now. You wait and see. Have you phoned Frank yet?" Vincent grunted that he was in the middle of dialling.

"Hello Vicar," said Frank cheerfully, "My back's still fine."

Vincent cut him short. "Frank, there's bad news, the fat lady sang...," Vincent took a deep breath. "Not Mildred Masham, what's happened to her?" came the concerned response.

"No, no Frank, it's Cuthbert. He's dead."

It is recorded in the book of Revelation that there was silence in heaven for half an hour. After a similar interval, during which Frank's mind went whirring Vincent knew not where, he responded, "Poor Daisy, she depended on him. What can I do to help? You'll have my full support." Vincent felt arrows of Christian love go out to this man who was now his senior churchwarden.

"Thank you Frank, I'll need a lot of help with the service — it'll be a big one, he's got six brothers. They'll all come to make sure."

"And what about the cross? Why don't I get Croft & Son to remove it before the rest falls down and crowns someone. It won't cause such a stir now. We could get old Man croft to accidentally lose it." Vincent quivered in terror at the thought of going against the council decision. It was too early to stop living in fear of his recently deceased bogeyman.

"Oh, I don't know Frank."

"Right, I'll take that as a 'yes' unless you say no," replied Frank, recovering his cheerfulness.

Somewhere deep within, Vincent remembered that in the days before a thousand defeats and disappointments, he had had the courage of his convictions and did what was right whatever PCCs said.

"No, I'll take the decision, Frank, go ahead and do it." Vincent slammed the phone down before he could change his mind.

Swivelling round, he crashed into big Mildred Masham, who sometimes wandered into the vicarage without knocking, on the assumption that her one pound a week covenant to the church made her a part owner.

"Is it true Cuthbert Grimshaw's been taken ill?" she asked after Vince had bounced off her, "I've been singing with the group and Madge said she saw the ambulance."

Vincent looked at her in a funny way and said without thinking, "Ill enough to be in Mortuary Ward at Eastern General." Mildred gasped and said, “Poor Daisy, she depended on him. I’d better go and tell the others.”

Among the wagging tongues of Yawtown, Mildred’s was the biggest, so Vincent knew that Cuthbert’s demise would be common knowledge within the hour. He sorted out Janet’s medication and set off to see Daisy. He arrived just after Lee, knowing that poor little Daisy would be in bits and pieces. He was thinking how best to help her through the arrangements.

“Hello Vicar,” she said, “Can I give you this? It’s the service details. I thought Cuthbert would take his leave of me like that one day, so I planned ahead. You’ll find the hymns and readings all typed up. I’ve told Berry & Burnham to arrange the service for Thursday lunch-time, if that’s OK with you, in church at noon, then a burial in the new part of the graveyard.” Vincent felt he heard Lee humming softly “Do not forsake me Oh my darling’” but decided he must be mistaken.

“Do feel free to sit down and have a good cry,” said Lee, utilising his counselling training from college.

“I’m not the crying sort, son. He had his threescore years and ten and died happy with a kipper in his mouth. It’s the vicar I feel sorry for.

I know he depended on Cuthbert, he'll leave a big hole at St Agatha's."

"Huge," agreed Vincent. "It won't be the same without him."

"Neither will the council office. He was always down there complaining about something. He liked a good row, it got his 'agremilins' going."

"Yes, I know love" said Vincent and he began to slip away as fast as he could.

Old man Croft was a splendid sight.

With his white beard and long gnarled fingers he looked like the grim reaper himself. He wanted to retire from the family business doing odd jobs in churches, but his two sons were both pushing sixty and wanting to retire themselves. So he kept the family business going as best he could. He listened patiently to Frank Williamson as he explained that the cross over the chancel steps needed to be removed. However, just as Frank was explaining that the job could not be done on Thursday lunch-time as there was a funeral, the radio announced the result of the 3 o' clock at Kempton.

"Thursday lunch-time was that?" checked the old man, "OK, leave it with us, Bye."

Cuthbert's funeral was proceeding smoothly. Vincent did not feel up to doing the funeral talk, so Lee Green was the preacher. He dabbled somewhat in flattering circumlocutions. Lee remembered Cuthbert as "stron- minded" whereas most people there knew perfectly well he was pig-headed. He had been "courageous in speaking out for what he believed in" whereas everyone knew he was a bully trying to get his own way. But Lee had done a reasonable job, and Vincent was beginning to relax and to think his colleague would make a vicar yet. As he announced the prayers, Janet began making spluttering noises on the back pew. Vincent thought she was gasping for breath and having one of her turns. He decided to lead the prayers from the back and check her out. One of Janet's hands left her mouth and pointed in the direction of the tower over the chancel. Vincent looked up to see the emergency door open from the inside and a gnarled hand on the end of a long white beard reach out to grab the broken cross and pull it in.

"That cross moves over my dead body," gasped an apparently overcome Janet as she struggled out into the porch to recover. Sometimes it is an advantage to have no sense of humour, so Vincent was able to continue with decorum when happier men than he would have broken down completely.

Berry & Burnham's men were ageing and had recently invested in a trolley on which to wheel their customers to their last resting place. Vincent solemnly led the procession out of church and along the path to the newly consecrated part of the graveyard, a fine stretch of ground leading down to the River Yaw at the bottom.

At the top of the slope, Mr Berry himself tripped over a curbstone and two of the bearers went to lift him up. The remaining two smiled a 'When will the old buffer give up and retire?'smile to each other and lifted their eyes to the heavens. The heavy coffin slid from their momentarily relaxed grip and the trolley began to gather momentum down the new path. Vincent, turning to see what was happening, was hit firmly in the groin by his enemy for the last time and fell writhing on the floor. The trolley gathered pace until it hit the low wall on the river bank.

As it stopped abruptly, the coffin shot off, launching itself onto the river, and floated merrily downstream between the pleasure boats. Daisy hooted with delight. "Ooh, he always wanted to be a sailor," she shouted in excitement.

The oldest brother said, “We came to make sure Cuthbert was properly buried and we’re not going till he is.” So, with a little help from the boatman, Berry & Burnham recovered their client, and a bruised and crouching Vincent finally laid his bogeyman to rest.

Chapter 3

◆

Occasionally, when relaxed and feeling confident, Vincent could be an impressive preacher. Unbeknown to Vincent, the vicar of St Bartholomew Oldtown had visited St Agatha's one Sunday and heard him on a good day. Vincent had no idea his fellow-divine had paid him a visit until he had been rung up and invited to be a visiting preacher at St Barthlomew's. Vincent had been flattered, and accepted immediately. Unfortunately, the visit was three days after Cuthbert's funeral. Vincent was still recovering from the blow in the groin from the coffin, and his preparation had been less than adequate. But doggedly he struggled out in the car in good time to reach the unfamiliar territory of Oldtown.

Vince was not the best map reader in the world when all was calm, and this week of all weeks his concentration was not of the best. He drove into Oldtown, and around Oldtown, and out of Oldtown, and back into Oldtown, and round and about Oldtown as half past ten grew closer and then passed. Vincent broke out into a cold sweat. He was close to total panic. In a final act of desperation, Vincent prayed. "Take me Lord, take me to St Bartholomew's. Show me, do I turn right or left?" The Lord seemed to say, "left", and there, ahead of him, appeared a large Anglican church. At last, St Bartholomew's.

"Thank you Lord," breathed the man of God, who had heard that the Lord always found parking spaces for charismatic Christians but had never felt he did the same for his sort.

The service, of course, had started without him. Vincent slipped into the vestry, changed into his robes, and slid silently into the empty curate's stall next to the choir during the prayers. The vicar then announced the hymn before the sermon. During the last verse, Vincent ascended the pulpit steps fervently thanking the Lord for his new found mercy and compassion on his lapsed map-reader-servant. Thus inspired, Vincent preached his sermon. Freed from the stares of the 'Cuthbert Crowd', Vincent felt a new man, and delivered his message with an enthusiasm he no longer felt capable of in front of his home crowd. Feeling uplifted and pleased, Vincent accompanied the local vicar down the aisle in the procession at the end of the service.

"Wonderful sermon,", said the vicar out of the side of his mouth, "but who are you?" Vincent gauped at him for a moment. "This is St Bartholomew's isn't it?" he enquired desperately.

"No, it's St Barnabas's," hissed the vicar.

"Oh hell," blurted out Vincent far too loudly for clerical decency.

"It's been an interesting morning," mused the vicar of St Barnabas's, as they reached the West door, "but what do I do with these?" He flicked his own redundant sermon notes in the air in a fit of mild hysteria.

"There's always next week," offered Vincent unsteadily. "My wife says, there's always another chance, it's never over till the fat lady sings."

At that moment, a young lady came up to Vincent and said hello. Her name was Ruth and she had been much taken with Vincent's sermon.

She was serious, even grave, and her large eyes and academic manner suggested to Vincent an intelligence unsettlingly greater than his own. Vincent enquired whether it had been his reference to the Old Testament sacrificial dealings with goats that had caught her attention. He had particularly relished that part of the sermon.

"Oh no,"' she replied, "It was the bit about your wife. You know, you apologised that she couldn't come with you to meet us because she had bad arthritis, but she would be praying for us. I thought, 'If I had bad arthritis, I'd be mad at God, not praying for other people.' She must be somebody special, and I'd like to be special too. What do I have to do to be a Christian?"

Vince was seriously taken aback. His usual post-service conversations were handling complaints about the omission or inclusion of certain hymns, and he wasn't emotionally prepared for a heartfelt response to Jesus Christ. He referred the nice young lady to her local vicar and watched them getting on well together.

His colleague took him by the arm as he walked him back to his car. "The Lord works in a mysterious way his wonders to perform," he mused, "You may have a very special gift, why don't you go cruising every Sunday and bump into different churches? It certainly breaks the boredom. But I'll follow Ruth up, I think she's genuine."

Over lunch, a shamefaced but somehow elated Vincent related to Janet the story of his morning, and she broke down into hysterical laughter yet again. Vincent nearly saw the funny side, but really would have preferred to be taken seriously by his partner in the gospel.

"Let me show you to your bedroom, I wouldn't want you to end up stretched out in the kitchen," giggled Janet, as she ushered him off for his customary Sunday afternoon survival snooze.

Just as Janet and Vincent sat down to tea, the phone rang. It was a Mr Henry Forth and he had an unusual request. "I've recently had my right leg amptutated," he began.

"Oh yes," responded Vincent, attempting his 'interested' voice.

"Yes, and I want it to have a good Christian burial in the family plot in your graveyard. The rest of me will be joining it eventually, and I'd like the whole of me to face the Maker together."

Vincent did not think this would be possible.

"Excuse me, but do you wish to be responsible for me having to hop in the after life?" asked Mr Forth aggressively. Vincent tried to explain that Christians believed in a spiritual resurrection body, not the old one cobbled together, but Mr Forth was having none of it.

"I ought to warn you that if you refuse to bury me in my own plot in your graveyard I'll report you to The Big Yawn."

'The Big Yawn' was the local name for Yawtown's local scandal sheet. As always, Vincent gave in to the blackmail.

"I'm perfectly willing to pay full funeral fees, but make it a proper service at the graveside mind. See you Wednesday at 10.00," said Mr Forth as he rang off.

Strangely, Vincent no longer felt like eating his now cold tea, and he felt most peculiar at evensong.

Wednesday came, and the mourners, led by Henry Forth himself, pushed in a wheelchair by his wife, assembled. Berry & Burnham arrived with a ludicrously thin coffin muttering, "Rum do this, rum do." Mr Berry kept eyeing Mr Forth oddly. He was not used to his clients chatting away during their own funerals. He was still recovering from the shock of checking out the coffin and finding it inscribed ‘Henry the Forth Part 1’.

“Queer do this, Vincent, queer do,” he muttered as he handed over the fee.

“Nowt queerer than folk,” responded Vincent with a grin. “He’s promised to leave the church a legacy.”

Mr Berry looked at Vincent with severe disaproval. The service continued, Mrs Forth had a good cry, and ‘Part 1’ was given a solemn burial.

“Thank you very much Vicar,” said ‘Part 2’, shaking his hand warmly, “I’ll be joining the leg in due course and I think we’ll be quite snug in there together.”

Bending down, Vincent spoke kindly to him and said, “When that happens may you rest in ‘pieces’... er... ah.. peace.”

Fortunately, Mr Forth laughed and announced he would be coming to church next Sunday to pay his respects in the usual way.

“Rest in *pieces*,” chuckled Mr Berry on his way to the limo, ‘Rest in pieces’ — it’s a goodun that, and I thought he had no sense of humour!”

HENRY THE
FORTH
PART I

Chapter 4

◆

The following weekend was harvest. On the Saturday, Vincent had an attack of harvest gloom. Being charming to those women who mucked up his nice church with flea-ridden flora was getting harder every year. And he found it increasingly distasteful to celebrate the bounty that enabled big Mildred Masham to gorge herself to an early heart attack, while Africa starved. Yet gamely in he wandered.

Mabel and her ladies were steadily immersing St Agatha's in horticulture. From font and frontal draped the dreaded grapes. As her fingers worked, Mabel's mind, such as it was, attempted golden thoughts. She began by praying for her priest, but quickly ended puzzling over the difference between a vicar and a rector. She began by recollecting last Sunday's Bible reading, but quickly realised she had forgotten the name of the eagle thing it was read from. It was on the tip of her tongue as the object of her spinsterly devotion shuffled by.

"Oh Vicar," gushed Mabel, "would you have a look for me? I'm so pleased with the grapes I've arranged dangling from your rectum." Glancing involuntarily behind him for a moment, Vincent panicked and fled. *The poor reverend*, thought Mabel, who was not a PCC member, *he's so upset at losing Mr Grimshaw he doesn't know what he's doing.*

The next day as he announced the opening hymn, Vincent's eye began to roam over the congregation trying to work out if any of them had ever done even once what the hymn apparently maintained was normal.

"Number 483," he announced, "We plough the fields and scatter the good seed on the land."

His eye landed on Fred Williamson, Frank's brother. Fred was a semi-retired shopkeeper who always went to Blackpool for his holidays and hated Germans. He wouldn't know what a plough looked like, but would certainly have complained if denied his chance to sing *Wir pflügen und wir streuen* on harvest Sunday. Over the years, Vincent had noted that when Fred sang hymns, only the lips moved. Fred never smiled in church, only in the pub. During the sermon, Fred would set his face in concrete. The preacher's jokes would always fall on stony ground near Fred. Fred would just about join in the liturgy, but with an economy of effort born only of long practice. When the others shared 'the peace', Fred would flag up the 'don't touch me' vibes. When there were guitars in church the other week, Fred had walked out. Fred would exude self-righteousness while putting a one pound coin in the collection, but be visibly annoyed when children disturbed the calm of the service. Fred never spoke to teenagers and never stayed behind for coffee after services.

Vincent's eye moved along thankfully to brother Frank. Frank's whole body was quivering as he sang, "All good gifts around us are sent from heaven above." He liked traditional hymns, but he still tapped his foot and went with the rhythm of the modern stuff. Frank had a radiant smile in 'The Peace', even when attempting to share it with Fred. He always looked at the preacher in the sermon, and he always said the liturgy with confidence. The part of the congregation surrounding Frank always seemed more alive and involved than the part around Fred. When there were guitars in church the other week, Frank had been playing one. Frank kept sweets and a *Thomas the Tank Engine* book in his pocket to amuse small children with, and he kept inviting the teenagers to tea at his house. Vincent wondered whether, in their long years together at St Agatha's, Frank had attracted more people to the church than Fred had put off. He decided it was probably a high scoring draw.

Vincent's eye swivelled round to Mabel Brook, known as Babbling Brook to Frank, but Vincent was unaware of this. In fact, Mabel was altogether a mystery to him. He wished he knew what went on in what passed for her mind. In fact, when the vicar prayed, Mabel would think, *What a wonderful voice he has*. When Mrs Pumfret read the lesson, Mabel would think, *What a vile dress she is wearing*. When Mabel sang the hymn, "Consubstantial coeternal while unending ages run", she would never wonder what it meant. When Mabel said the confession recently, she had remembered she hadn't turned on the oven for the Sunday roast. When the vicar read the banns of marriage, Mabel would spend the next ten minutes wondering whether Tracy Williamson of this parish was a Frank Williamson Williamson or a Fred Williamson Williamson. When Lee preached, Mabel would sulk because he was not the vicar. When Mabel went up for communion, she would admire her altar flower arrangement. Immediately afterwards, the other week, she had walked purposefully past the sidesmen to activate her oven before it was discovered she had left undone those roasts which she ought to have done.

Next to Mabel was Maggie Fisher. Maggie was also a mystery to Vincent, but a warm glow enveloped Vincent as he looked at someone he sensed was a devout and caring Christian. Little did he know that when he said the prayers, Maggie habitually prayed for Janet, either stuck at home ill or on the back pew in pain. When Mrs Pumfret read the lesson, Maggie would avert her gaze from the ghastly dress by following the words in her Bible. When Maggie sang the hymn "Consubstantial coeternal while unending ages run", she would ask Lee Green over coffee what it meant. She was as surprised as she was baffled by the answer that it was the Anglican alternative to transubstantial and co-substantial. She had thought it may have been something to do with the police force. When Maggie said the confession she would pour her heart out to God about how impatient she had been with her sick mother, and she would ask his help for the future. When Vincent read the banns, Maggie knew Tracy was a Frank Williamson Williamson because she went to Frank's home group. She was sad because Wayne Parsons of the parish of St Saviour's-by-the-Sea only knew Jesus as a swear word. When Lee preached, Maggie winced but still revelled in the idea of Jesus as her Good Shepherd who knew her by name and led her to green pastures. She took communion as medicine for her soul and prayed that Jesus would still be with her when she took lunch round to Mum later.

"Freds and Franks," mumbled Vincent too audibly as they sang "And, what thou most desirest, Our humble thankful hearts." *Maggies and Mabels*, he mulled, *mixed bunches in churches, mixed bunches — Lord preserve us!..* "Would the mixed bunches please bring up the children's gifts now?" he announced, saw the confusion, and tried again, "Would the children's bunch now please bring up their mixed harvest gifts," and this seemed to do the trick.

The service proceeded up to the point Vincent had been dreading — the notices. It was Janet who had nerved him up to this, and she was sitting there looking at him. There was no escape. "Strike while the iron is hot!" she had counselled. "Just tell them, Don't ask the PCC's permission, you'll get away with it now that Cuthbert's gone.

Remember — if it's announced, it's in the programme. You announce and I'll pray. I'm sure this time God's going to do something big." In fact, she had been up half the night praying while Vincent snored, and was now paying the price in the agonies of her joints, but she began to pray again as Vincent fought his way against his better judgement to the microphone.

Usually, the solid citizens of St Agatha's day-dreamed happily through the notices as messages about autumn fairs and harvest gifts wafted over their heads. But now Vincent really caught their attention. Big Mildred Masham's lower jaw hung open a great distance from the upper like a whale straining plankton. Fred Williamson appeared to examine his shoelaces intently, while muttering something unrepeatable about the vicar's sanity, but fortunately only those within three pews of him knew this.

It wasn't quite as bad as the time Vincent had announced sharing 'the peace' for the first time. At least on this occasion there was no Cuthbert Grimshaw. And, for the congregation, the ridiculous embarrassment was not immediate. There was still time to arrange a late holiday or to fall ill. A hundred brains whirled into overdrive, and satisfied smiles began to lurk behind grave exteriors. Numerous grandchildren and widowed mothers from Wick to Torquay were about to receive unexpected visits. A private nursing home nearby did not yet know of its boost from NHS queue-jumpers with suddenly urgent hernias. Usually unimaginative businessmen planned sales drives to Sweden and Scunthorpe. For the Reverend Vincent Popplethwaite was unexpectedly talking the biggest embarrassment of all. Evangelism.

Usually, Vince's Sunday elocution was smooth and grave — a genuine "This is the Church of England addressing an official communiqué to the Almighty and he better be listening" voice. But if he got flustered and out of liturgical mode, he became all squeaky and dithery. Vince duly squeaked and dithered as he sensed a seismic reaction.

Apparently, the Bishop was putting pressure on St Agatha's to "do something" before the frightful Decade of Evangelism was over. Vincent had agreed to one of the Bishop's pet ideas. St Agatha's was to have a "visiting week". All the congregation were expected to visit people they didn't know, or, even worse, people they did know, to tell them about God, or, even worse, Jesus, and to invite them to a "guest service". The crowning blow was that the Bishop would be the preacher and he would take special note of those who did, and did not, bring a victim for his evangelising zeal. St Agatha's prided itself on being a proper Anglican church, and held the Bishop, unlike its vicar, in some awe. Anyone turning up alone would endure the shame of failure, anyone actually turning up with a victim would endure far worse from the sharp tongues of the Red Lion and the Rotary Club.

St Agatha's was about to be either branded by its shepherd in the no-hopers zone, or stranded in the no-comfort zone. It was Catch 22, and catch any train or plane would do. At last, Vince dithered to a dreadful close, and normality resumed as they sang the comfortable old hymn "And we, shall we be faithless? Shall hearts fail, hands hang down? Shall we evade the conflict and cast away our crown?" *Yes, yes,* shouted a hundred inner voices.

Mr Broadhead had come to St Agatha's all his life, starting as the bellows boy for the old organ. This had been on the small balcony at the back of church, and the balcony was where Mr Broadhead sat to this day. No matter that nobody else came to join him in these days of smaller congregations, and no matter that he was getting infirm and the stairs were rickety, the balcony was what Mr Broadhead came for and the balcony was his resting place. Today, being harvest, an overspill from downstairs had joined him, but he had secured his usual seat at the front just ahead of them in a tight race. Here he could lean heavily on the balcony front as he snoozed through the sermon.

But Mr Broadhead had a secret. At least he though it was a secret. He was bald. Some years ago, he had invested in a wig that he fancied made him look twenty years younger. The trouble was that the wig looked so artificial, so transparently what it really was, that the whole of Yawtown knew his secret.

As Vincent began his harvest sermon, Mr Broadhead began to feel even more sleepy than usual. His head slumped forward on to the balcony front. Slowly at first, then with gathering speed, the wig began to slip across his forehead. Mr Broadhead slumbered on. At last, it broke free completely, and floated gently down to the pews below. Vincent gazed at it in fascination, but continued his sermon. The wig landed on Mabel Brook's lap. In a trice, Mabel sized up the situation. She glanced to her right. She was sitting next to Maggie, who had hair down to her shoulders. She glanced to her left. There sat a gentleman called Kevin Jones. Kevin and his wife were in church for the first time in their adult lives, attracted to the harvest service by a leaflet pushed through the letter box. Kevin had recently been promoted to a white collar job, and was trying hard to put an irresponsible youth behind him. He was determined not to make a fool of himself in church, and was watching what others did before committing himself to standing, sitting, passing the collection plate, and so on. Kevin was not yet quite thirty, but his hairline was rapidly receding. Mabel glanced up at his balding visage, knew it was her duty to minimise this stranger's embarrassment, and thrust the wig firmly on his unsuspecting head.

To say that Kevin was surprised would be an understatement. He was thunderstruck. But, equally, he was determined not to make a fuss and only do what the others did. He stared ahead fixidly for a moment or two, feverishly sizing up the situation. He had been trying to join the Freemasons, and the thought occurred to him that there were many strange rituals in the world. He had heard the vicar say it was time to pass the plate, but perhaps he had misheard and he had actually said, "Pass the pate." Kevin congratulated himself on his calmness and quick-thinking under pressure, reached over his wife, and planted the wig firmly on Fred Williamson's head.

To say that Fred was not amused would be an understatement. He was thunderously annoyed, and started calling Kevin names. Kevin instantly regretted his rash move and prayed with urgent conviction for the first time since his pet hamster was ill: "Save me, get me away from this man!" Vincent had arranged for the Bible reading to come half way through his talk, to make the point more clearly. He announced the reading, and a seething, bad-mouthing Fred Williamson was forced to abandon his persecution and march to the front to do the reading.

Perhaps there is a God after all, thought Kevin. Fred realised half way up he was still wearing Mr Broadhead's wig and flung it off in disgust. Kevin looked further round and was impressed that several people seemed to be sobbing deeply, while desperately trying to hold themselves in check so as not to disturb others. Even his wife was affected. He decided it must be a deeply emotional experience to come to church, and that these brave, distraught souls were being immensely thoughtful holding themselves in check. Fred began to read from Matthew chapter 10 verse 29:

> "Are not two sparrows sold for a penny? Yet not one of them will fall to the ground apart from the will of your Father. And even the very hairs of your head are all numbered. So don't be afraid; you are worth more than many sparrows..."

Kevin decided he had better take religion seriously for a while.

At the end of the service, Lee Green went up to Mr Broadhead to return his much-travelled wig and to offer comfort and reassurance. He explained that it was perfectly OK for Christians to wear wigs because, after all, they were in the Bible. "Even Moses wore a wig, you know," he said brightly.

"How do you know that, then?" enquired Mr Broadhead suspiciously.

"Well, sometimes he went about with Aaron and sometimes without Aaron," responded Lee.

Mr Broadhead was just about to tell the young man not to take the Micky out of him, when a nice young lady who had been sitting behind him butted in, "My name's Ruth," she said, "And I'm a nurse. Would you like me to help you get the wig back on securely?"

"Oh, thank you very much dear," responded the old man, brightening considerably, "Do you come from round here?"

"No, I come from Oldtown but I've just started at Eastern General, I met your vicar last week and thought I'd try his church."

Mr Broadhead was loving all the unusual attention, and, by the time several other people had come up to his balcony to wish him well, he was having a wonderful time.

"I don't think I'll sit there again," he told them.

"Thats right," said Ruth, "you sit with the others downstairs."

"Oh no, replied the eternal bellows boy, I'll sit on the back row up here. Then I'll be safe!"

Meanwhile, Vincent was talking with Mr Forth, who had kept his word and turned up with his wife.

"Poor Henry," she said, "he's got to go to the dentist tomorrow to have a tooth out." Vincent quivered and shook in alarm. "Don't worry, Vicar," she smiled, "Henry says we can let the tooth fairy take care of it." Vincent silently blessed the tooth fairy and asked Mr Forth what he had thought of the service.

"Well, this whole business has really made me think. I've been very impressed by your kindness and the service this morning, and I wanted to thank God that most of me was still here. I thought your visiting week was a very good idea. If you don't keep putting fresh coals on the fire, it goes out doesn't it! So I asked God to say if I should go and tell my pals about the Bishop's guest service. And he did, so I'll have to won't I!" He laughed.

"How did God tell you that?" asked Vincent, fascinated.

"That last hymn, Vicar, it were just for me — how did it go? Oh yes, 'Go forth and tell, O church of God arise'." Henry Forth's never had a more direct order than that.

Over coffee, in the hall afterwards, talk was all of deeply-missed grandchildren, of lonely widowed mothers, of urgently-needed operations, and the size of the Swedish market.

Maggie Fisher had a shrill and penetrating voice. She was not aware of this and would have been horrified to have been told, but she was slightly deaf and was determined to hear clearly whatever it was she said. She was talking to, or perhaps at, Frank Williamson.

"The vicar's right you know," she shrilled. "Where would Peter have been without Andrew?" Andrew, after all, had been the one who introduced Peter to Jesus.

Uncrucified, thought Frank with a sinking feeling, remembering where the introduction had eventually lead the big fisherman.

"I'm going to invite Mrs Finnigan," Maggie continued, "you know, her who lost her husband, lives opposite Berry & Burnham. I'll ask her round to coffee on Tuesday and pop the question. Who are you going to ask?"

Frank, loyal churchwarden that he was, was no evangelistic storm trooper. He had been undecided between the hernia and Scunthorpe. But then, in one of those life changing-flashes that afflict even normal people, he remembered how God had kept him going when his first wife had died.

"I've decided to ask my new mother-in-law," he replied, feeling like Sydney Carton in *A Tale of Two Cities*. "We're asking her to stay for a few days."

A funny silence descended on the hall. Hernias healed. Sweden shrank. In the distance, the youth group could be heard practising for the evening service and singing out of tune, "I will build my church, and the gates of hell shall not prevail against it."

"Even St Agatha's Lord?" whispered Vincent nervously.

"Especially St Agatha's," replied a small voice inside his head.

"What will you build it with?" asked Vincent, looking round at his mixed bunch.

"Just the usuals," replied the voice. *"The prayers of the people and the suffering of the saints."*

Just then, Janet hobbled in, having finished her prayer stint at church. "How's it going dear?" she asked brightly.

"Pretty well, I'm afraid," replied her reluctant hero. "Would you like your cup of Fairdoos, or would you prefer coffee instead?"

Janet hit him with her stick and said, "Meet Kevin and Miranda, they're new and they've had a very interesting morning."

Chapter 5

◆

Lee took the youth service that evening. The youth group still sang "I will build my church" out of tune, but Lee was banking on the theory God didn't mind it out of tune as long as they sang it.

Fred, however, had a different theory. "I came back tonight because I needed a proper service after that shambles this morning, and I find it taken over by spotty youths who can't sing. You've ruined evensong, you have. We used to have a robed choir chanting proper canticles and now you have kids off the street with no reverence and even less harmony. I've had enough I can tell you. Next week I'm off to St Mark's. Only saving grace was the sermon wasn't too long. At least you don't keep us sat for ever missing our suppers like the vicar does because he's lost his way in his notes."

The truth was that Lee had a three-point sermon but, as he got to point three and kept stammering "thirdly", his notes had disappeared. He had scattered the lot with a dramatic hand movement at the climax of point two, and the sheet had fluttered down from the pulpit and disappeared through a hole in the floorboards. Eventually, the organist had whispered, "'Thirdly's' through the floorboards Reverend," and Reverend had called it a day.

Sensing from the begrudging thanks for brevity a chink in Fred's hostile armour, Lee enquired, "Is it a Prayer Book evensong at St Mark's, Sir?" Fred liked the word "Sir" and replied, "Of course it is, and nothing missed out. The last time I went a couple of years ago it was balm to sore ears." Unusually for him, Lee omitted to point out that balm is for lips, not ears, and respectfully made a request: "Could you take me with you next week, Mr Williamson? I need to broaden my experience and I'm not terribly familiar with the Prayer Book evensong... unfortunately," he added, quietly, "it could be balmy to my ears as well," but Fred didn't quite pick up the whisper.

"Alright, lad, I'll pick you up at ten past six," responded Fred, taken aback with the wild thought that Lee might be teachable after all, if only he could be exposed to Cranmer's glory. "But no comments while it's on, and then we'll see how you liked it."

"It's a deal, Mr Williamson, thank you, I'm sure it will be a very interesting evening," replied Lee, full of respect.

Next Sunday, Fred picked Lee up and drove across town to St Mark's. Cars were parking everywhere, and there was an impressive line-up of motor bikes in the small church car park.

"It looks very popular," said Lee, sounding surprised, "I expect people flock from miles around to hear Cranmer these days as he gets rarer." Fred grunted and began to look worried.

He was slightly reassured by the sidesman on the door, immaculate in a five hundred pound suit and a public school accent. "Hello Lee," he said, "How's life at St Agatha's?"

"Varied, Mike, varied. Meet Fred Williamson, he's brought me along tonight."

"I'm delighted to meet you Mr Williamson," he said, gushing charm and enthusiasm, and shaking him firmly by the hand. Fred suddenly had a twinge of recognition of that posh voice.

"Have we met before somewhere?" he enquired.

"Well, now you mention it, I think you came up before me when you refused to pay that parking fine Mr Williamson," smiled Mike. Lee was also smiling, but Fred bolted into the church, and Lee quickly chased him.

Fred sought anonymity in a lengthy head-bowed prayer, but eventually he came up for air. He began to look around. What he saw, his senses refused to believe. The normal uniform was black leather, and the normal hairdo was pink with green stripes, and the normal age was nineteen, but the variety was vast. However, it was safe to assume that, among the congregation, only Fred had done National Service and been proud of it.

"Peace and love, Lee," said a not completely youthful hippy on the pew behind. "Who's the old guy?"

"Meet Freddie, Flowerboy," said Lee, "he's kosher."

"Joy Freddie!" beamed Flowerboy. "Have we met before?"

"I seriously doubt it," glowered Fred.

"Got it! Hernia!" said Flowerboy in triumph. "I saw you at the clinic last week. I'm doing your hernia on the private next Wednesday. You won't recognise me because I don't wear my ordinary clothes at work. Health and joy Freddie - see you Wednesday!"

Lee whispered to a mortally shocked Freddie, "Sorry about the throwback - I think the people here have problems with him. Is he really doing your hernia?" Fred indicated that he was no longer quite so sure. They looked around again in wonderment.

"Pretty serious amplifiers for Cranmer, Mr Williamson," muttered Lee eventually. A girl in black leather and orange hair sat next to Fred. Leaning over him towards Lee, she said, "I've got the yellow dog collar in the bag, Big Rev. Will you introduce me to your dad?"

Before Big Rev could respond, the recently appointed vicar of St Mark's appeared at the front, wearing a rough brown cassock and a radio microphone. "Hi, I'm Dave," he blasted out, cheerfully. "Let's start with the 'Reykjavik Wave'." Everyone except 'Freddie' stood up with hands high in the air, waving them from left to right one after the other to form a wave going through the congregation.

"Welcome to 'Dave's Nave Wave Rave'," he boomed. "Main notice is that next week it's an evangelistic guest service, so bring your friends to 'Dave's Nave Wave Rave Save'! The current Omega course is full, but a new one starts next month. The first fifty get the places! That's where you'll really meet the greatest social revolutionary the world has ever seen, but he's here tonight too. Let's worship Jesus."

At this, the lights went out, a huge wall of amplified heavy rock hit Fred's ears, and Orange Hair got up to join her friends dancing in the cleared area at the front. A complex set of images began to play on a giant screen, projected from a large set of slide projectors in the balcony. Strobe lights began to play on the dancers and the congregation. Even Fred's hair became pink, orange and green for split seconds at a time. Fred decided he had died and gone to hell. "If only I'd been more like Frank," he lamented.

Eventually, the cacophony capitulated, Orange Hair read a Bible reading, Flowerboy led some prayers, and Mike the Magistrate preached a wonderful sermon about repentance and forgiveness during which Fred's emotions became as putty in his hands.

"Thank you for coming," said Dave the Rave Rev at the end. "Remember — Jesus Christ, mainstream man he ain't. He invented counter-culture. Mainstream man stocks up on mainstream jerseys in his mainstream wardrobe next to his serious sock space. Jesus the counter-culture man said if you've got two jerseys give one away to someone without any. I've got friends in a serious jersey shortage situation in Yawtown. They're in the bed and breakfasts, and the Sally Army, and the cardboard corner down by the station. So, if you've got clothes in the wardrobe at home, how about sharing what you've come in with the cold and hungry and homeless? There's a jersey collection point in the porch on the way out. Thank you!"

Lee stripped his jersey off and placed it on the pile just above a five hundred pound suit. "I wonder what Mike's going home in?" he mused out loud.

"The Jag as usual," beamed Mike, appearing in borrowed track suit bottoms and Savile Row shirt.

The cold wind bit into Lee's body as he emerged, jerseyless, into the night air. Fred had emerged, joyless, just in front of him.

"You've got to hand it to Cranmer, Mr Williamson, he was way ahead of his time," was all Lee managed to say before Fred sprinted for his car and disappeared into the traffic. Lee's teeth chattered all the three miles home, but he thought to himself that the fun had been worth every shiver.

Strangely, Fred never again threatened to leave St Agatha's for a proper church and he began to see Vincent in a new light, as the last bastion of normality against the onrushing tide of orange hair and Lee Greens. He even began to support Vincent on the church council, but Vincent never knew why.

Some months later, when Vincent was giving lunch to one of his regular tramps on the doorstep, he caught sight of the name tab which was peeling away from his jersey. It said "Fred Williamson" and Vincent thought, *What a coincidence, a tramp called Fred Williamson. Wait till I tell Frank!*

Chapter 6

◆

The alarm clock clattered into Vincent's brain midway through its grand finale to the night's dream programme. He was being consecrated Bishop of Batley — the culmination of all youthful ambition. At the climax to the ceremony, just before the actual consecration, the Archbishop had finally looked at him straight in the eye, and realised the dreadful mistake. "I didn't mean Vincent Popplethwaite of Yawtown," he boomed, "I meant Bultmann Popplethwaite, Professor of Liberal Deconstruction at Nietzsche College, author of 'The Bible as Pamphlet'. Get rid of the bumpkin!"

The clattering continued carcophanously in the cavity of his cranium. Crawling towards the clamour, the confused cleric clicked the klaxon switch that completed the capitulation of his clanging gong. The angry Archbishop zoomed away into Bultmannian oblivion.

"I know I'm a bumpkin," Vincent muttered blearily to his luminous green digital clock, "but at least I'm God's bumpkin." He prayed his usual first prayer, "Lead me where you want me today, Lord," and donned his carpet slippers.

Big Mildred Masham knew Vincent's most intimate friend only as "That Vicarage Dog", but somehow Vincent still managed to call him 'Charger'. Charger was a golden retriever, well meaning but dim as a retarded dodo and timid as a tortoise with claustrophobia. Vincent let the sad brute into the enclosed garden and returned to the bedroom to dress while Janet slumbered on. The most memorable advice his vicar had ever given him as a curate had been, "Never let them catch you without your shoes and dog collar on, always put them on first thing." Thirty years later, Vincent obediently slipped on his clerical shirt, his dog collar and his shoes. As he reached for the trousers, he glanced out of the window just in time to see Charger push his way through the vicarage hedge and out to freedom in the 'undogly' world beyond. The scent of the latest potential girlfriend heralded on the morning breeze had been just too much for him.

Immediately, Vincent raced downstairs, threw on his full length winter coat and screeched out of the drive in the Escort estate in hot pursuit. He turned one corner, and then another, but still no sign appeared. Finally, he turned into Grace Avenue, and there was the beast, trotting along the pavement sniffing the offerings of a rival defecator as he went.

"Thank you Lord," whispered the new recipient of the Lord's grace. Vincent careered to a stop, opened the tailgate, grabbed the surprised beast from behind, threw it into the car and slammed the tailgate down upon it.

As Vincent walked round to the driver's door, he noticed a large, red-faced man running at him and shouting, "Hey, thief, leave my dog alone." Vincent looked at the captured retriever. It was similar to Charger, very similar, but its coat was shinier and it looked altogether more groomed and handsome.

"Let my dog out of your car," boomed the man. "Do you know who that is? That's Frederico Confetti the Third, won second prize at Cruft's last month."

Vincent apologised and explained about Charger. Just then, he caught a glimpse of another retriever, just turning the corner ahead into Hope Street. Frederico Confetti quite liked the tailgate of the Escort and had to be dragged out by his owner before Vincent could roar off in high temper after Charger.

Charger wandered into a front garden full of large bushes, and cocked his leg up on one of them. Vincent ran out of the car and caught him in a rugby tackle. There was a brief struggle, but Charger was no match for Vincent, and he was duly dragged and carried into the tailgate. As he slammed the tailgate down this time, Vincent suddenly felt better. A small victory had been won against the quirks and chaos of his life.

He suddenly realised that, in the struggle, his own dog collar had come off. It was still very early morning and the whole street seemed fast asleep, so he confidently returned to the garden to retrieve his collar. As he did so, an ambulance siren could be heard in the distance, quickly getting louder. The front door of the house opened as the ambulance came to a smart stop just behind the Escort. Vincent hid behind the bushes and held his breath.

"Come in," said the lady at the door to the ambulancemen, "but I'm afraid it's too late." Vincent waited until they had all gone inside, and sneaked out to his car. As he got to the car, an ambulanceman ran out of the house to collect some equipment and the lady half followed. "Vicar," she shouted in surprise, "How good of you to come, how did you know? do come in!"

Vincent smiled and did as he was told. He realised that the lady was Grace Newton, a slightly eccentric middle-aged hairdresser whom Janet had known as 'Amazing Grace'. Grace had stopped coming to church a year ago. Vincent assumed it was in protest at the drums Darren Clarke had played in the youth service. Vincent didn't have the courage to visit her to confirm his theory. In fact, Grace's elderly and ailing father had come to live with them, and she felt she couldn't leave him on a Sunday morning. She was feeling terribly guilty about this, but didn't have the courage to contact the vicar to explain.

"What's happened, Grace?" asked Vincent, recovering at least part of his composure.

"It's Daddy, he's been going downhill for a while, but I think he's had a heart attack in the night. It's so good of you to come at this hour, can you come and say a prayer with us?"

The ambulanceman explained gently to Grace that there was nothing they could do for her father now. With quivering lips, she led Vincent and her husband Norris up to Daddy's bedroom. Vincent knelt at the bedside, commended the old man's soul to God, and prayed sensitively for Grace and Norris. Their tears came as Vincent hugged them and encouraged them to touch Daddy's cold face and hands. Grace held her father's wrinkled and emaciated hand and said, "He used to play the organ at St Wilfred's you know. He hasn't been to church for years, but look, he was reading his Prayer Book last night."

"He looks very peaceful now, doesn't he?" said Vincent.

"Yes, but the real Daddy's not in this body any more is he?" replied Grace.

"No, he's gone on his journey to God," responded Vincent, "and we can trust God with him now. He loves him every bit as much as you do. And you don't get to heaven by going to church, you just have to trust."

"You've been such a help and comfort," said Norris as they returned downstairs. "Come in the lounge, take your coat off, and have a cup of tea."

Vincent was just about to do so when he remembered his trousers, still on the bed at home.

For a few moments, Vincent was all 'Ers and Ahs'. Eventually, he said, "I think I'd better get back to Janet now, but I'll call again later in the day when I've got my trou... er... my diary on me and we can talk about the funeral."

"What a wonderful man," said Grace to Norris, and Norris nodded. "I still don't know how he knew, I wonder if God told him in a dream or something? It'll be wonderful to get back to church again."

"I think I'll come with you from now on," said Norris as he waved the vicar off.

"Oh, Vicar," shouted Norris as Vincent opened his car door, "I wonder if you could keep a lookout for our dog. It's a golden retriever and it seems to have escaped in all the commotion."

Vincent released Tricksy round the corner and decided he hoped that Charger had been humanely destroyed by a number 11 bus on the High Street. But oh the joy and relief when he got home to find his pet snoozing by the vicarage garage!

Chapter 7

◆

Janet was creaking around downstairs all of a dither. She had seen the trousers. In fact, she had gone through Vincent's wardrobe and counted the trousers. All of them. Even his summer shorts. Every single pair was there. For a moment, she wondered if the second coming had happened and Vince had been taken as he dressed and she had been left. Then she noticed Charger had gone too, and began to discount the theory. The car arrived back, and in strolled Charger, followed by Vincent looking strained. "I need a large mug of caffeine, I mean coffee," he announced, "I'm off upstairs to finish getting dressed."

As Janet got the story slowly out of Vincent, she cackled away merrily and said, "Well, that makes a wonderful start to my prayer day." She had set aside the day to pray for the forthcoming visiting week and the Bishop's guest service. "I promise I won't tell my ladies. They'll be arriving soon for the 'Prayer and cream Cake' meeting. I think I've finally found a format to attract them out to pray. I'll make an appointment with Amazing and invite her while she does my hair. She's got the salon next to the 'Fair Shares' shop. I can get my hairdo and my 'Fairdoo' at the same time!" Vince grunted that they would be about as good as each other, when the doorbell rang.

For the next ten minutes, Janet sat in state in the lounge, receiving, while Vincent answered the door and acted as butler. First in was Maggie Fisher, then came Mabel Brook with Frank's new wife, Mary, then a group of ladies together, and then came young Ruth, a little shyly, but determined to join in for a few minutes before going on shift. Finally, in came Lee Green, who said to Ruth, "Oh great! You did come. Where are the cream cakes?" and did his best to sit near her. Vince was not allowed to join in the prayer time because Janet sent him out for more cream cakes, but it seemed to him as he got back that it had gone very well indeed. The cakes were voted a success, even when Charger stole Miss Pumfret's cream slice from between her fingers and got banished to the kennel. Vince was very moved when Maggie said a prayer for Janet before they all left.

"I'll have to find out where Ruth is living and pay her a visit," Vincent mused to Lee. "12 Nightingale House," replied Lee. "It's quite a nice flat. I think she wants to get confirmed."

"Oh, well done, Lee," said Vincent, but Janet just smiled at them both.

The morning of the Newton funeral, Vincent pottered about St Agatha's with Ron the verger getting things ready. He had a fine pair of wooden trestles that he put out by the chancel steps ready for the coffin. Ron couldn't stay for the service as he had a dentist's appointment, so he called out, "I'm off now Vicar, see you Sunday." He absent-mindedly locked the vestry door as usual and wandered off wondering how much it would hurt.

Vincent finished fine-tuning the exact placing of his much loved trestles, and returned to the vestry to put on his robes and find his sermon notes. When he found the door locked, it gradually dawned on him that his own keys were inside, that the only other person in the building was Mildred Masham the reserve organist, and that in five minutes a large funeral party would be arriving. Vincent glowered at his new enemy the door and began to kick it. It was a solid door and unyielding. Then Vincent had a flash of inspiration. He went to the organ, asked Mildred to stop playing for a moment, and showed her the locked door. After the incident with the runaway coffin at the Grimshaw funeral, Mr Berry had quietly retired the oldest of his retainers and secured the services of a very efficient young man called Paul Slade. As Vincent consulted with Big Mildred by the vestry door, young Mr Slade marched in with the 'Berry & Burnham' tressles, put the rickety-looking old wooden ones to the side, and placed his trestles in what he thought was a nice spot. As he did so, he was startled to hear a tremendous thud coming from the direction of the vestry. The ground shook as though there was an earthquake, followed immediately by a final bang and shriek of triumph. Mr Slade returned to his clients as Vincent slipped his gardening trousers inside his cassock and walked gravely out to meet the family.

Walking alongside Mr Berry, Vincent reached the door of the church and began to speak the time-honoured sentences. As he did so, he saw to his amazement and displeasure that his trestles were gone.

" 'And Jesus said...' who moved my trestles?... er... 'I am the resurrection and the life...'." Vincent recovered himself and reached the front. He peered at the coffin as young Mr Slade positioned it correctly. The name plaque seriously worried him. It said, "In loving memory of our dear mother, Nora Peabody". Vincent walked even more gravely over to Mr Berry. "You've brought the wrong coffin," he hissed, "Nora Peabody is tomorrow." Mr Berry went white and fainted on the spot. Vincent announced the first hymn and had a serious word with young Slade. At the end of the service he announced that the hearse had some mechnical trouble and would need to divert to the garage on the way to the Crematorium.

Vincent had never ridden in so slow a limo. Nor such a roundabout route to the crem. Eventually they arrived, just before the hearse and the now-switched coffin.

"It was a wonderful service, so quiet and dignified, so calm and reassuring," said Amazing to Vincent.

"We'll see you on Sunday when the Bishop comes," added her husband as the party shook hands. Vincent never saw the efficient Mr Slade again, but was interested to see the oldest retainer again the following day when Nora Peabody came round for her second send-off.

"How's it been going then Vincent?" asked the Bishop over coffee at the vicarage.

"Rather well I think. We've suddenly got some new people coming, and our folk have quite surprised me — a lot of them have been asking their friends and I never thought they would!"

"Power of prayer," grinned Janet, "we've been doing overtime recently."

"I gather your churchwarden died suddenly a few weeks ago," said the Bisho.,

"Yes," responded Vincent, brightening up a lot, it's since then that things have been happening."

"Oh dear, a blessed subtraction," smiled the Bishop.

Janet hobbled off to the kitchen. The Bishop whispered to Vincent, "I'm worried about Janet, she seems a lot worse than last time I saw her." A cold flannel seemed to hit Vincent's mind as he was reminded of the great threat to his current warm spiritual glow. He had a sudden glimpse of a future he didn't want to meet.

"She spends too much time praying and too little time at the doctor's," he explained, "I don't know what to do with her."

Frank and his team were beginning to have a hard time. Mr Broadhead was wandering about at the back of church like a chicken without a roost because all the seats on the balcony had been taken while he was saying hello to Ruth. In fact the only empty pews at the moment were the front ones. Then Henry Forth arrived with his wheelchair and his friends.

"Meet the club, Frank," said Mr Forth warmly, "they've all come!" Frank gazed at the long line of wheelchairs and crutches and enquired if it were the 'failed kickboxers' club.

"This is The Yawtown One-Legged Club," he responded, "Where can we go?" The sidesmen huffed and puffed and dragged the front pews to

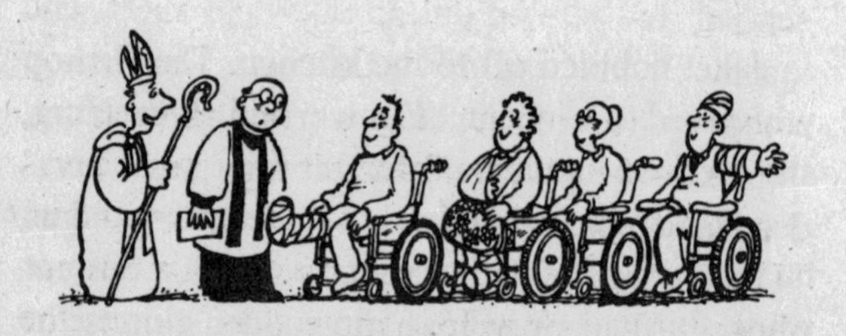

the side to make way for the wheelchairs and their occupants.

"You'll notice," said Frank to the Bishop in the vestry, "That we've been to the highways and byways and compelled them to come in, but some of them put up a hell of a struggle." The Bishop looked at the splinters all around the vestry, the shattered door frame, and the bits of an old door piled in one corner, and said, "Whatever happened to this door?"

"It's time to pray now Bishop," responded Vincent quickly.

As the procession reached the chancel, the Bishop and Vincent gauped in astonishment at the halt and the lame filling the front rows. It looked like the casualty department on a very bad Saturday night. Vincent noticed Ruth fussing among the chairs making everyone comfortable. He welcomed everybody, mentioned that the service was printed out on a special sheet, and that the Bishop would now take over. The Bishop stood up to commence the opening greeting, "The Lord be with you", but his microphone was dead and no one heard him. He shouted out, "There's something wrong with this microphone." Vincent, whose mind was still on the wheelchairs, responded immediately in his loudest voice with the opening response, "And also with you."

After a moment's horrified, embarrassed silence, Henry Forth and the Bishop both burst out laughing at the same time, and everyone followed suit. Lee Green stopped helping Ruth with the halt and the lame and returned to his proper job of running the sound system. This time he switched the Bishop on. The Bishop thought, *I've underestimated Vincent, he's got a really sharp sense of humour and it seems a really happy church.* The Bishop relaxed and tried a few of his old jokes. The packed congregation warmed to him, and the service started going really well. As the Bishop got up to preach, Vincent suddenly felt a profound awe as the presence of God seemed to envelop him.

"Strength for today and bright hope for tomorrow," said the familiar voice inside his head as Vincent received what appeared to be the divine prescription for his needs.

The Bishop's main theme was the resurrection.

"Death is something everyone has to face, both the death of our loved ones and the certainty of our own death. We can't beat it by ourselves.

But Jesus has beaten it for us. The way to beat death is to trust in him."

Vincent looked round his congregation at Henry Forth, with one leg already buried, and at his club members who had each had their brush with death, at Amazing and Norris Newton fresh from the funeral, at Daisy Grimshaw outwardly perky but inwardly desperately missing Cuthbert, at Frank Williamson whose own first wife had died only four years ago, at Ruth who was struggling in a ward for the terminally ill, at Mr Broadhead in the loneliness of his old age, at Mrs Finnnigan from opposite Berry & Burnham sitting with Maggie and still grieving for her husband, and at all his mixed bunches.

Finally, he spotted Janet, looking old and weary tonight, and he wondered for the very first time how much longer she was for this world. *Go for it Bishop*, he prayed, *This is what it's all about, sock it to them*. The Bishop duly socked. Finally, he invited anyone who wanted to make a new start with the Saviour from death to take a booklet from him at the end of the service.

The line-up for the booklet was long and impressive. It is surprising how aggressive people in wheelchairs can be when it comes to queues, and five of the first seven had only four legs between them.

"I wasn't sure whether to come to you or not," explained Henry Forth, "until the last hymn, and that clinched it."

"How do you mean?" asked the Bishop, intrigued.

"You asked whether we would be ashamed to be known by the name of 'Christian', and I realised I would be a bit. But then we sang, 'Forth in thy name oh Lord we go,' and that was Henry Forth's answer! I'll have to answer to the Lord's name from now on won't I?!"

Chapter 8

◆

Vincent had had a heavy day visiting some of the new people. Munching his third Mars Bar of the day, he pulled up at church, glanced nervously round to see if anyone was watching him, pulled up his coat collar to avoid recognition, and furtively slipped into St Agatha's. Moments later, another figure, mysterious in the twilight and a broad-brimmed hat, slipped in behind him.

"Eating many of those are you?" asked Frank, as they walked down the aisle in the dimness.

"They keep me going," grunted Vincent, "I haven't had time for a meal today. Too many visits. And I'm still behindhand. It's all those new people."

They arrived at their destination.

"Do you think anyone's noticed?" asked Vincent nervously.

"Not that I know of," Frank reassured him confidently, "and they never will — not at an inch a week." With an expertise born of six weeks' practice, they together half lifted and half shoved St Agatha's large, free-standing pulpit an inch nearer the centre of the building. Frank carefully arranged the dust so as to disguise the move. The pulpit had been half behind a pillar, way to one side of the church, and very hard to see from the side where the 'Cuthbert Crowd' sat. Vincent had asked the PCC to move it to the centre. Cuthbert had opposed him on the grounds that the pulpit had always been there, and the PCC voted to keep it where it was. Now, riddled with guilt and fear, but egged on by an irresistible Frank, Vincent was moving it an inch a week.

Vincent sat on the front pew with a sudden chest pain. "Are you OK?" enquired Frank, concerned.

"Yes, just a bit of wind," replied Vincent, "I think I need the toilet." Vincent toddled off to the vestry toilet.

Suddenly, with a mighty crash, the porch door was flung open and something very large came towards Frank in the darkness, every footstep making the ground shake the whole length of the church. Even Frank started to feel nervous and his face went bright red.

"Oh, it's you," said Big Mildred contemptuously. "What are you doing here?"

"Just one or two jobs with the Vicar," smiled Frank.

"Ah, so that's what he's doing instead of visiting now is it? Handyman stuff in the dark?" sniffed Big Mildred.

"What do you mean by that?" enquired Frank, stiffening in defence of his friend.

"He hasn't been to see my mother in six weeks, I really don't know what he does with his time. He hasn't visited me for over a year! What's that?" she added, pointing at a large, round object she had just spotted in the gloom.

"It's a drum," replied Frank evenly, "The music group are playing on Sunday morning."

"Music group? More like the 'nasty noise group'. It shouldn't be allowed in church. Where's the vicar? I want a word with him about it."

"In the toilet," smiled Frank.

"I'll wait for him, then."

Vincent, of course, had heard every word. He decided to stay in the toilet. While Frank pretended to be busy, Mildred waited with arms folded while Vincent quivered in hiding. He knew he hadn't visited Mrs Masham for six weeks, because he'd had all the new people to deal with, and the guilt was gnawing away at him anyway. So he didn't feel he could cope with Mildred at the moment. Eventually, Frank took his courage in his hands, told Mildred the vicar wasn't feeling too well, and ushered her out through the porch door.

"I'll see him on Sunday," she boomed as she left.

"Thanks Frank. She's in a fearful mood isn't she?" said Vincent timorously as he emerged.

"Never noticed the pulpit though," replied his friend, smiling.

"Well, I've just got one more visit before I go home. I used to visit the widow ten days after a funeral, but I haven't got round to Mrs Simpcock for four weeks. I must go today."

"Why?" asked Frank, reasonably.

"Er... it's what people expect," dithered Vincent, "I'll see you Sunday, Frank."

Mrs Simpcock didn't seem too pleased to see Vincent, but she invited him in anyway.

"How are you feeling, then?" enquired the pastor. "Do you feel you're coming to terms with it yet? " "Great!" replied Mrs Simpcock. "I had a good policy on him, the money's come through, and I've just booked a cruise."

"Well, that's something very positive," said Vincent, interpreting her as sympathetically as possible. "Did you decide what to do with Bill's ashes? Do you want any advice?"

"Oh yes, they're over there." Vincent squinted in the direction indicated — shelves over the kitchen table. A ghastly forboding came over him.

"How do you mean?" he enquired apprehensively. Mrs Simpcock went over to the shelves and brought down a large new-egg timer filled with grey 'sand'. "Bugger never did any work when he was alive, so I'm making him work now," she explained as she flipped the timer over to demonstrate.

"I think I'd better be going now," muttered Vincent.

"Suit yourself," said Mrs Simpcock and let him out of the kitchen door. Vincent felt a peculiar turn come over him and had a sudden longing for Janet's reassuring arms. He put the car into the garage and shambled wearily into the house.

"Oh, you've come home," said Janet, frostily. "I thought you must have gone on a cruise or something. Your dinner's in the tramp who called half an hour ago and I'm off to bed."

Vincent was astonished. "Whatever is the matter Janet?" he asked.

"Have you ever been in the Johnson's house at number 15?" she asked. Vincent hadn't. "He's a decorator," Janet continues. "They've got paint peeling off the kitchen ceiling and no wallpaper at all on one room of the lounge. He's always decorating somewhere else. Goodnight."

Something died inside Vincent as silently he watched Janet struggle painfully up the stairs and bang the bedroom door. He half-emptied the whisky bottle, sat on his favourite chair, and had a serious case of the glooms. All those new people finding a faith and joining the church had been wonderful at first. He'd thrown himself into helping them to integrate, and all he'd got from the regulars was resentment that he wasn't spending time with them. And now Janet. It was hope that had died inside him. *For the first time in years, Lord, I'd had hope, but more people just means more problems and everyone resents me. I'm only trying to do my best, why does it always go wrong?* He felt like Elijah after killing the prophets of Baal when Jezebel threatened to kill him.

That night Vincent couldn't sleep properly. He had a recurring nightmare in which Big Mildred Jezebel leapt up in the middle of next Sunday's service, denounced the big drum and ran at him with a large dagger in her hand. Vincent got up, ate another Mars Bar because he was famished, and felt very, very sorry for himself.

Next morning, Janet was conciliatory, but Vincent was tense and tetchy.

What he needed was a large dose of caffeine with his cornflakes. Something had to hit his headache and hit it hard before it laid him out for the morning. Janet, gushing with concern, pressed a large mug of 'Fairdoos' decaff into his hand. He scowled and grunted, Janet turned away to the sink. Vincent quickly poured the useless liquid into the Yucca plant that loomed over the kitchen table. Janet went off to get dressed. Vincent went to the filing cabinet in the study and extracted his contraband from between 'Men's

Fellowship' and 'Mothers' Union'. He had carefully wrapped it in a label saying, 'Milk of Magnesia', but it was actually proper exploitative coffee with added addictive.

"Caffeine, caffeine," he mumbled as, at last, proper coffee met boiling water and lips met mug.

Janet returned and screamed. "Argh. What's that brown liquid oozing from the Yucca Plant?"

Vincent froze in panic. The trick had worked well for weeks now, but it was one 'Fairdoos' too many for the Yucca. At that moment he was rescued by his enemy. The phone rang.

"Oh, good morning, is that the vicar?" enquired a rather artificially plummy female voice. Vincent replied that he still was for the moment, and took a swift slurp of coffee. Some of it splashed on to the phone and he noisily wiped it away. "I'm so sorry," he murmured, "it's my caffeine of magnesia. What can I do to help?"

"I'm hoping you can baptise my son," replied the posh voice.

"Oh, congratulations," said Vincent, finally slipping into vicar-mode. "How old is the little chap?"

"He's twenty-one next week," came the reply. "We never got round to getting him done as a baby and I thought it would make a lovely twenty-first birthday present. Would it be possible to do it as a surprise?"

"A surprise?" asked Vincent, surprised.

"Yes, l would walk with him along the High Street and, as we got to St Agatha's, steer him into the church. You could christen him before he knew what was going on. It would make such a wonderful surprise birthday present, don't you think?"

Vincent gawped vacuously as Janet mopped the floor and he struggled to find a way of saying 'no'. Eventually, after a considerable pause, Vincent said, "No." It was the only way of saying no he had thought of. "You see, baptism is a serious step of joining the Christian church and taking a step of faith in God. An adult would need to go to preparation classes before deciding to get baptised."

"Oh," said Posh Voice, taken aback. "Have you got any then?"

"Any what?"

"Classes."

"Oh, well we have actually," said Vincent, remembering all the new people in his confirmation group.

"He would need to come round to the vicarage on Thursday at 8 pm."

"Right, I'll send him then," said Posh Voice, and rang off.

Vincent blinked into the middle distance in wonderment and began to smile.

"What was all that about?" enquired Janet. Vincent told her, and his smile got wider. Janet hooted with glee at the vision of Vincent lurking in the church porch with a hose pipe for his victim and the Yucca mess was quite forgotten.

Vincent kissed his wife on the cheek, normal life restored, and said, "I'm off to the 'Incontinental' Retirement Home ...with communion."

"Where?" asked Janet intrigued.

"The Continental Retirement Home," replied Vincent, all oblivious.

"I suspect you were right the first time," said Janet as he made for the garage.

Vincent was pleased to find a small table ready for him in the main lounge, and a fair-sized congregation. Some had been wheeled in in wheelchairs and left with the brake on. Others clearly didn't know what day of the week it was, but nevertheless it was a handy crowd. Vincent handed round service cards, and began. Halfway through the thanksgiving prayer which consecrated the bread and wine, Mrs Mather at the back leaned over to her friend Mrs Parkinson. Both were deaf and so Mrs Mather employed the world's loudest ever stage whisper, "Have you ever heard owt so boring?" Vincent stumbled for a moment but then carried on. Mrs Parkinson responded in kind, "I thought it was a concert".

Vincent continued manfully. When it came to the communion distribution, the residents came up with some novel things to do with the bread. On receiving the bread the correct response to the words, "The body of Christ keep you in eternal life", was "Amen". There were several cases of "Thank you very much dear"; one, "Are you Catholic then?" and two pieces of bread ended up in handbags. However, they all drank the wine, some of them enthusiastically, and Vincent had to consecrate extra wine twice. He became more and more distressed, and was desperate to clear up and leave.

Just before he could escape, a very elderly lady who had more or less behaved herself beckoned him over, "Could I have a word with you young man in my room?" Vincent swallowed hard and agreed. He and a nurse half led and half carried the lady until she was sitting on her bed. Her name was Mrs Forth.

"I think you've met my son Henry," she said. "He gave me this, and I've been reading it, I think it's very good." Mrs Forth showed Vincent the evangelistic booklet offering four steps to be coming a Christian that Henry had brought in. "He's walking again now on his artificial leg, you know," said the old lady, proud of her lad. "He had to keep both hands free in case he slipped and fell, so he brought the booklet stuffed into the hollow bit of the artificial leg. He had the devil's own job getting it off to give it to me!" she giggled.

Vincent never used evangelistic booklets because they made him feel uncomfortable, so he glanced through it, squirmed, and said, "What did you find so good about it Mrs Forth?"

"That bit where it said you could be born again and be like a new baby. That's quite an achievment at my age! How old do you think I am?" Vincent was used to this game.

"Oh, I should think about seventy."

"I'm eighty-eight!" she responded triumphantly. Vincent feigned amazement.

"You see my Henry's different now. Losing that leg knocked the stuffing out of him you know, but now he's got religion he's come round and he's lost his fear. So will you say a prayer with me? I think it's time I had God on my side, I'll be meeting him soon enough." Vincent said his prayer, Mrs Forth had a cry, Vincent stood up and knocked over a glass of water containing Mrs Forth's teeth on to the carpet, the nurse said not to worry she would clear it up, and Vincent retired home.

There at his desk he struggled with his sermon notes. Vincent always struggled with sermon notes because he had always been a plodder. Writing sermons inevitably awakened the vivid memories of school – the smell of chalk, the compass marks on the desk, the ink blodges on the white shirt, the essay that took him twice as long to write as anyone else, and, most chillingly, the comments he would get from Fat Joe that would certainly accompany his nine out of twenty.

Popplethwaite never uses one word where fifteen will do.	Bit wordy this morning, Vicar.
As much life in this story as the dodo's grandma.	Have you thought of having visiting preachers, Vicar?
You have serious gaps in your knowledge of grammar Write: 'A verb is a doing word' fifty times by tomorrow morning.	I'm sorry Vicar, I didn't quite follow you this morning.

Vincent had heard them all and each one still hurt. But yet, he knew that, if he sweated long enough at his desk, he could still preach a good sermon on his day. After all, he was the boy with no social life who had amazed Fat Joe with his six O levels.

So Vincent got stuck into the parable of the workers in the vineyard where the ones who were employed at dusk got the same pay as those who had slaved away all day. He was struggling to find an illustration for it when the phone rang and spoiled his concentration. He sighed and picked up the receiver.

"Forty-five per cent... er... 45713," he said."

"Hello Vicar, it's Henry here.

Henry sounded a bit choked up. "I'm just ringing to thank you for what you did for my Mother this morning."

"Thats alright, I enjoyed it," lied Vincent.

"Yes, she died half an hour ago, I think you'd got her ready."

Vincent was stunned. The old lady had seemed sparkly enough to keep going for ages.

"I'm so sorry Henry," he said.

"It's OK, it's for the best, she'd made her peace. Will you bury her in the family plot with my leg?" Vincent said that he would and Henry rang off.

Vince stared into space for a while, coming to terms with the news, and then returned to his problem. He was sure, if only he hadn't been interrupted, he would have found an illustration, but no inspiration came. So he wandered off to check the lunch-time post. As he opened a letter and began to read, his legs went to jelly, his face went scarlet, and he had difficulty breathing. He half fell onto the settee in shock and disbelief:

Dear Revd Popplethwaite,

We at 'Unmask' feel it is much more honest for leading churchmen like yourself to be open about their sexuality than to keep their 'gay' life secret. We very much hope you will have the integrity to 'come out' before others unmask you.

Yours in Christian Fellowship,

'Unmask'.

Janet hobbled into the room as the new found colour started to drain out of Vincent's face.

"I don't have any sort of a life, let alone a gay one," he mumbled as Janet took the letter and read it. Her jaw set firm and her eyes began to blaze.

"With fellowship like theirs who needs heathens?" she stormed. "I can assure them there's nothing gay about you, nothing at all. Anyway, what's this other letter, it looks very similar?" Janet opened the second letter and read it out to Vincent:

Dear Revd Popplethwaite,

We at Unmask would like to apologise for the clerical error made in sending you our recent letter. It had been intended for Rev. Bultmann

Popplethwaite, Professor of Liberal Deconstruction at Nietzsche College, author of 'The Bible as Pamphlet' and the next Bishop of Batley. Please accept our apologies for any inconvenience caused.

In Christian Fellowship,

'Unmask'

"Inconvenience," muttered Vincent weakly. "Does having a heart attack count as inconvenience?" He paused and reflected, remembering his dream. *So, it's better to be a bumpkin than a Bultmann after all. I bet it's a battle at Batley now. I think I'd better go to bed, I don't feel at all well.*

Vincent was still not properly well by Sunday morning, and every time the phone rang he had a new fit of the panics in case it was the press. He looked round the congregation in fear. What if they had been fed rumours about him? Suddenly, as he rose to announce the first hymn, he remembered another problem. There, sitting stone-faced just behind the drum kit was Big Mildred Masham. As she glowered at Jason the teenage drummer, Vincent couldn't work out whether she was willing him to play without making a noise, or to play so loudly she would get sympathy for the walk-out she was about to stage. Vincent swallowed hard and announced, "The first hymn is..."

"Excuse me vicar," interrupted Frank, "I've something important to say." Vincent froze, horrified. Surely Frank wasn't a member of' 'Unmask'? "We've noticed how long it takes to get the congregation out of church through the door at the back and decided to call a fire drill during a service. We'll be opening the front door as well, and I want everyone in the front pews to use it. Congregate on the side lawn and the sidesmen will time how long it takes. Right — FIRE DRILL!" Mildred, thwarted for the moment, stormed out of her pew just as Jason jumped up from the drum kit, stick in hand. The stick hit Mildred firmly on the forehead and she crashed down to the floor in the aisle. Fred Williamson called Jason something unmentionable, helped Mildred to her feet and ushered her out.

Moments later, everyone got outside, and then Frank ordered them back in. Big Mildred muttered to Fred, "Right, that's it, I've had enough of that place now, no more vicious nasty noise groups for me," and off she went. But everyone else was so busy getting out and then coming back in again that her departure went unnoticed.

Everyone was so careful not to give offence by sitting where someone else had been that it took a little while for them to be settled. But eventually Vincent was able to continue. "As I was saying, the first hymn is number 345... er... 'Light up the fire and let the flame burn'. Everyone had a good laugh and the service seemed to go really well after that.

At the end, a young man came to have a word with Vincent. "I think my mother rang you in the week," he said sheepishly. "I really enjoyed the service. I didn't realise you could have drums and good music in churches, I thought it was boring old organs and hymns. Could I join your classes on Thursday nights?" Vincent beamed and said he could. Just then Fred Williamson came up to him, his face flickering with fury. "You're destroying the church you are. You realise you've just lost Mildred Masham now. She'll be cancelling her covenant this week and then how will you pay the quota? You don't do that with spotty youths and drumsticks!" Vincent reflected for a moment on Mildred's one pound a week and decided he could live with the loss.

"She'll be a big loss," he said to Fred, "very big," and wandered off.

Vincent sank back into his armchair after lunch, emotionally exhausted. "Why have we got all these problems, love?" he asked Janet, plaintivley.

"It's simple," she replied. "First of all, growth means change and change always means conflict. Second, for the first time in years we're beating the Enemy, and he doesn't like it. We've got to pray harder. I'll get my 'prayer and cream cake' group on to it. And I've had an idea. It's getting quite full on a Sunday morning now. Why don't you have two services instead? One could be boring for the 'straights', and the other could be lively for the 'hallelujahs'."

Vincent protested that he couldn't cope with the extra work.

"Let Lee do more, and get the lay people involved in the services," she urged. It was all a bit much for Vincent so he said he would sleep on it, and went off for his Sunday afternoon snooze.

On the Monday it was Mrs Forth's funeral. The church heating system had broken down, but the verger had rigged up a calor gas burner just behind Vincent to keep his circulation going. He suddenly thought of his illustration to the workers in the vineyard story — Mrs Forth! "Why didn't I think of it on Sunday?!" he lamented. "Why am I always so slow?" So Vincent told the congregation about the story and about his visit to Mrs Forth and about how she had made her peace with God just before she died. "So we know that we can hand her over to God now with confidence. She left it a bit late, but she made it!"

Henry had asked for the famous passage about love from 1 Corinthians chapter 13 to be read out. It was his mother's favourite piece of the Bible. In fact, it was the only bit she knew. So Vincent read it out, swaying backwards to get some benefit from the heater. He had just got to the verse "If I surrender my body to the flames but have not love I gain nothing", when he smelt a pungent smell. Smoke appeared from behind his shoulder. Suddenly, he realised his surplice had caught fire behind him. Quickly he lay himself down on the floor and rolled over and over between the choir stalls. The congregation looked at him intently. Realising the fire was out and he was OK, Vincent got up, dusted himself down and carried on with the reading. Most of the congregation clearly thought this was part of the ceremony, and Henry was seriously impressed, "Marvellous visual aid to the reading, Vicar. Quite dramatic, it really brought the point home. I thought it was very brave of you. Very brave indeed."

Chapter 9

◆

Vincent had never had such a large confirmation group. There was Henry Forth and his wife, with three of Henry's one-legged friends, Ruth and a nursing friend of hers called Vicki, Kevin and Miranda, Frank's new mother-in-law, who seemed to have taken up residence with them after the guest service, Amazing and Norris, Mrs Finnigan and her friend Doris, Darren Clarke and his two friends from the 'nasty noise group', two

girls from the youth group who seemed to be 'nasty noise groupies', and Timothy Jenkins, who had just escaped baptism by surprise. Finally, there were two young men whom Henry hardly knew — Simon and Peter.

"What brought you to the confirmation group then Simon?" essayed Vincent.

"It's the funniest thing," replied Simon, "I'd never given God a thought since the day I prayed I'd win the conker competition and my prize conker got smashed in the first round. But I woke up in bed a few weeks ago suddenly desperate to know God. And there was a voice inside my head saying 'It's time to forgive me for the conker'. I couldn't get God out of my mind so I rang you up and here I am. And the other thing is, I'm a pharmacist at the hospital and I met Ruth a few weeks ago and there was something special about

her that she had and I wanted it too." Lee suddenly looked at Simon rather sternly, and Ruth blushed.

"That's wonderful," said Vincent, "and what about you Peter?"

"That's amazing," said Peter. "I'd looked at most religions but none of them did anything for me. But I'd never looked at Christianity. Then one night I woke up in bed and this huge angel burst into my room. It told me to serve Jesus and to find a vicar who could tell me what it was all about. I know I wasn't dreaming because the bedroom door was closed to start with and wide open when the angel had gone. Oh, and I'm a junior doctor at the hospital and when I saw Ruth the other day I noticed she had an angel standing next to her. Crazy isn't it? So I asked her if she went to church, and here I am. Lee's face was a wonderful mixture of astonishment, pleasure and horror, as he stared at Peter. Ruth blushed again and smiled at Lee reassuringly.

Vincent was beginning to feel out of his depth so he said a prayer and began the discussion. The subject tonight was 'the ten commandments'. Henry Forth was a study in concentration as Lee read the passage from Exodus chapter 20. When he finished, Henry sighed and said, "Well Vicar

I've just added up that I've broken nine of those in my life. Am I in trouble then?"

Vincent, shaken, thought for a moment. "Let me just check on number six," he responded.

"That's the one," confirmed Henry, smiling.

"Excuse me, what's number six and why hasn't Henry tried it?" enquired Mrs Forth.

"Thou shalt not murder," confirmed Lee.

Looking stonily at her husband, Mrs Forth retorted, "Well, speaking personally, number six is the biggest temptation of the lot!"

"We are in trouble if we break the ten commandments," Vincent began, hesitatingly, because he knew what he believed but was nervous of saying it. "God has given us rules to live by, he's told us what's right and what's wrong and if we want to follow him, we have to live his way. But because Jesus has died for our sins we can say sorry to God and he forgives us. So you're in trouble until you say sorry and mean it, and then you're OK as long as you try to live God's way in the future. And you aren't any different from the rest of us. I break number four every Sunday. Twenty pairs of eyes started scanning Exodus chapter 20 for Vincent's Sunday vice.

"But what you do isn't work, Vicar," said Amazing Grace reassuringly. "It's a way of life, and you've got the other six days to have a rest in." Vincent suddenly emphathised with Mrs Forth's temptation, but his emotion was cut short by an indignant outburst from Peter.

"But that's not what you said in your booklet! In your booklet you said that we can't have ethics cast in tablets of stone, that it's OK to live together as long as you respect each other, that God made men with a roving eye and there were worse sins in the book, that coveting your neigbour's manservant is pretty harmless really, and life would be deadly boring if we really didn't do all the things the Bible tells us not to do."

Everybody looked either at Vincent or Peter open-mouthed. Vincent's gaping jaw pointed in the direction of Peter. He knew that he had never written a booklet in his life and that it was highly unlikely anyone would ever ask him to.

Then Vincent had a rare brainwave. "What booklet are you thinking of?" he enquired.

"This one, I picked it up in Yawtown library between 'Christianity' and 'Other Religions'," he replied.

Vincent looked at the title. *The Bible as Pamphlet by Bultmann Popplethwaite, Professor of*

Liberal Deconstruction at Nietzsche College. Vincent smiled in relief. "It's quite a coincidence really, but it's a different Popplethwaite. He's Bultmann and I'm Vincent and I'm not clever enough to write booklets. But I do believe the Bible and I do think that, if God tells us something is wrong, it's always wrong whatever the spirit of the age we live in."

"Hear! hear!" shouted Frank's new mother-in-law, "I'm glad there's still at least one vicar we can trust to stand up for right and wrong." And to Vincent's relief and pleasure, the others agreed.

"I suppose," Henry summed up, "if you're going to be a Christian you'd better be a proper Christian and sign up for the whole lot. When I signed up for the army, I signed up for square-bashing as well as rifle shooting, and I couldn't pick and choose which orders I liked. I had to obey the lot."

Even Peter was relieved, "You see Rev. Popplethwaite,"

"Call me Vincent," interrupted Vincent pleadingly.

"You see, Vincent, this angel told me I had to be saved. But that booklet says we don't believe in judgement and hell anymore, and that God doesn't mind much whatever we do. He's into toleration not judgementalism. So I couldn't find anything to be saved from. And tonight you've talked about right and wrong and judgement and being sorry and being forgiven, and you've told me what to be saved from. Thank you."

Vincent was quite overcome. "I know I'm dull and old fashioned, and I'm just a bumpkin at the side of these professors, but I think I know what being a Christian is all about."

Just then, the phone rang. It was Ron the verger. "That lot have been at it again, smoking in the hall, playing with a 'weeji' board, and they haven't paid the rent for six months now." Ron was referring to The Ladies' Club that hired the hall on a Monday.

"Thanks Ron, I'll write them a last warning letter tomorrow," said Vincent, and returned to the group.

At the end, Vincent had an 'any questions' time.

"What I don't understand," said Frank's new mother-in-law, is how they managed to carry the ark around with them. You know, they carried it into battle and put it up in the Temple. But it was huge — four hundred and fifty feet long. How could a few priests carry it around?" Vincent's brow furrowed, but Lee spoke up, "Two arks Mrs Jones, two different arks. Noah's ark was the big one, and the ark of the covenant was what they carried round. That was just a box. By the way, when God told all the animals to go forth out of the ark and multiply, why did the two snakes stay behind?"

"I don't know young man but I think we're about to find out," responded Mrs Forth thinly.

"They were only adders," responded Lee gleefully. "And do you know what sort of angels they were, Peter? — Arkangels!!" Lee hugged himself in delight while the rest groaned.

The group began to go home, saying what a good time they had had and how they would see each other next week.

"I think we should all go out two by two," said Lee, "to avoid muggings. "Simon and Peter, you should definitely stick together, and I'll make sure Ruth gets home safely."

"Actually I thought I should take Vicki home," responded Simon and Peter in unison. So Vicki took them both with her to Nightingale House before going on duty.

Vincent, elated with the evening, went off to find Janet, who had been resting. After her 'prayer and cream cake' meeting that morning, and another prayer stint for the confirmation group, she had been exhausted and taken to her bed. She was gasping for breath and unable to talk. Her face seemed a little more contorted than usual and one arm didn't seem to work properly.

"Oh my darling," gasped Vincent, "I'll fetch Doctor Little."

Janet knew Doctor Little as 'Doctor Do Little' because he never seemed to summon up the courage to act about anything, but Vincent still had complete faith in him simply because he was a doctor, and Vincent believed doctors always knew best.

After what seemed like an age Doctor Little arrived and examined Janet.

"I think we should have you in Eastern General for a while to check you over," said the doctor, surprising even himself with his decisivness. He summoned an ambulance and, with dread eating away into his heart, Vincent followed in the car. By the time he found the ward, Janet was in bed and asleep. A nurse was with her.

"What's the matter with her nurse?" asked Vincent nervously. The nurse looked astonished to see him, and suddenly he realised it was Vicki.

"I think Janet's had a slight stroke — the doctor will be along in a moment to have a look at her," she responded. A young doctor came up to them, talking as he walked, "Is this the new admission, nurse?" He examined Janet for a few moments. "Is this your wife, sir?" he asked Vincent without looking up.

"Yes, Peter, it's Janet," replied Vincent. Now it was Peter's turn to be astonished at the role reversal.

"Oh, I'm sorry, hello again Vincent. I'm afraid she might have had a slight stroke. Could you explain to me what she was like when you found her?" Vincent did so.

"Well, she's comfortable now and we'll see what she's like in the morning. Hopefully, it won't have been too bad." Peter then stared at the end of the bed as though he had seen a ghost. "Can you see that?" he asked Vincent, incredulously.

"What?" asked Vincent, bemused.

"The angel standing at the foot of the bed as though it's guarding it."

"The only angel I can see is in the bed," responded Vincent gloomily.

Vincent sat with Janet for an hour or so, occasionally holding her hand, more for his comfort than hers. Eventually, Vicki suggested he go home for a few hours' sleep.

"I'll keep an eye on her through the night," she reassured him as she ushered him out of the ward. Exhausted and wretched, Vincent returned home to a stiff whisky and a welcome greeting from Charger. The events of the day crowded his mind as he tried to sleep. He'd never thought much about angels before and wasn't quite sure what to make of Peter and his sightings. Were they worrying or comforting? At last he drifted into a confused dreamland of confirmation groups and hospitals, of joy at seeing God at work, and horror at what God was allowing to happen to his beloved.

As he awoke, Vincent instantly remembered last night and the thrill of horror came afresh. This was one nightmare he couldn't wake up out of. Fearing he had overslept, he stepped immediately out of bed and fell over the prone body of Charger, measuring his length on the bedroom floor. Vincent called him a stupid brute, and then realised that he normally slept in the kitchen, and must have joined him for comfort's sake in the absence of Janet.

"Come on, old friend, let's get some breakfast," said Vincent, more kindly, as the pair wandered down the stairs.

As they got to the hall, the phone rang.

"Hello Vicar, it's Maggie here. We've heard about Janet. We wondered if you would like me to go to the hospital during the afternoon to sit with her, and Mabel to come and do some chores at the vicarage."

Vincent was not normally good at receiving help, but he was still too sleepy to resist and thanked Maggie for their thoughtfulness. He put the phone down and it rang again. This time it was his aunt.

Ermintrude Popplethwaite was as formidable in life as was her name in print. Vincent had been terrified of her from the tender age of five. He had gone to stay with her for some reason, and she had suddenly hit him on the cheek and said, "That's for nowt so don't do 'owt." Her ascendancy over Vincent, thus gained, had now lasted nearly fifty years.

"I've heard about Janet," said Aunty, "So I'm coming over to make sure the vicarage runs smoothly. I'll arrive about 3 pm." Normally, Vincent would simply have said "Thankyou Aunt Ermintrude", but this morning the worm finally turned. Perhaps it was the thought of an intruding Ermintrude fighting with Mabel for domestic control, or perhaps it was his repressed anger at what was happening to Janet coming bubbling out.

"I've already made arrangements, Aunty, so I won't be needing you thank you. I'm more concerned about Janet than the house— I must get ready now to go and see her. Goodbye."

Vincent replaced the phone quickly before she could respond, and it rang as he put it down. He unplugged the thing and shambled into the filing cabinet for his 'Caffeine of Magnesia'. Thus fortified, he dressed and drove to Eastern General with hope and fear battling with each other in his imagination.

Janet was sat up in bed, drinking a cup of tea, and smiling radiantly at the lady in the next bed.

"Hello my love, how are you? I hope I didn't frighten you with my turn," she said, as Vincent approached. Suddenly, the relief poured over him, the events of the last few hours overpowered him, the sudden awaking caught up with him, the bump on the head from falling over Charger registered with him, and Vincent fainted across the bottom of Janet's bed.

Chapter 10

◆

Two nurses helped Vincent to a chair, where he sat dazed and feeling foolish. Peter walked in, looked at the end of the bed, and said, "That's funny, the angel's gone."

"The way Vincent fell over it, I'm not surprised, poor thing," retorted Janet, as she giggled. Eventually, Vincent felt restored, and he and Janet were left alone for a chat.

"You've got to take things easily and look after yourself," Vincent counselled.

"I'll be as sensible as I can," replied Janet, "But I can't give up now that we're winning after all these years. I know I can't go on for ever, but I've still got some use left in me. I'm not giving up yet, I'll keep praying and working to the end. It's never over till the fat lady sings and she hasn't sung yet."

As usual, Vincent felt powerless to argue, but he did recount his triumph in repelling Aunt Ermintrude. After a while, Maggie arrived and Vincent returned to the vicarage to catch up on paperwork.

As Mabel cooked and cleaned, Vincent wrote his promised letter to the 'weeji' playing Ladies' Club. One more incident of rule breaking, smoking, or 'weeji' playing and they would no longer be able to rent the hall.

There was then just time to get to church and move the pulpit another inch before people started arriving for the funeral of a lady called Grandma Higgins. It was raining quite hard so Vincent took his umbrella with him to meet the family at the church porch. Grandma's two daughters, Hilda and Hazel, had neither brollies nor hats, so Vincent gave them his umbrella for the long walk through the graveyard to the church.

"Give the umbrella to the verger when you get to the church," he whispered to them. As he reached the door, Vincent felt a tug at his surplice. He looked round.

"Who do we give it to?" hissed Hilda.

"I said the verger," hissed Vincent back. He straightened up to commence the first scripture sentence as Ron acquired the brolly.

"The verger said, 'I am the resurrection and the life...'" Ron gave him a very strange look, but he kept going oblivious.

At the end of the service, Ron told Vincent what he had said at the beginning. At first he was quite offended. But then he cracked a little, and said that it had made him think.

"I've never been quite certain, Vicar, whether Christ was the resurrection and the life for me. And it's about time he was. Is it too late for me to join the confirmation group? I've never been confirmed before you know!"

Vincent, amazed, said he was most welcome, but he had better go now before the cortège left him behind.

Running, Vincent leapt into his car and did a racing start to catch up with the procession of cars heading for the burial ground at the town crematorium. Ahead of him, the hearse and the first few cars got through the lights, but he didn't. At the next junction, unbeknown to Vincent, another procession turned to follow Grandma Higgins. As Vincent turned at the lights he was relieved to see the hearse ahead, and followed it to the crem.

Leaping out, he mingled with the mourners, searching for Hilda and Hazel.

"Hello Vincent," said Father O'Brien brightly. "So you've started pursuing good Catholics to the grave now have you?"

"I'm looking for Grandma Higgins," said Vincent, looking round wildly.

"Well this is Eileen O'Grady, and she's always had a Catholic priest so far," smiled Father O'Brien. "Why don't you try the burial over there?" he said, pointing to a group of figures in the distance. As Vincent scurried off, the Father shouted after him, "Make sure you don't fall in today, the flask's empty!"

"What a wonderful man," said Hilda to Hazel, "He's gone to comfort the other party as well."

"I'd like to ask him," said Hazel to Hilda, "Who that verger is who's the resurrection and the life."

"That's the Verger Mary," said Hilda to Hazel, employing her best religious voice. Vincent arrived and the burial commenced. Afterwards, Hazel tackled him on the 'Verger Mary' and Vincent quickly got out of his depth.

"Why don't you come to our group next week?" he suggested, "You can ask your questions there." To his amazement, Hazel said she would love to, and Hilda begged to be allowed to come too.

A couple of days later, Vincent drove to Eastern General to bring Janet home. He had hated being without her, and his heart was happy as he turned the car into the High Street. Ahead of him was a large 'Yawtown Gazette' newspaper board. Its headline read: ANGRY VICAR SACKS HIS LADIES.

"I wonder what that's about," he mused. He tried to work out which of his neighbours could have got into trouble. Suddenly, his jaw opened, he emitted a strangulated cry, and his foot went flat on the brake. The car stopped suddenly, but not as suddenly as the car following him. Front bulbs met rear lights, and bits of glass and Perspex splattered over the High Street. The driver of the following car stormed out, screaming abuse at Vincent, using imaginative and unrepeatable adjectives to describe Vincent's special brand of idiocy. Finally, the driver looked at Vincent, still cowering, shocked, in his seat.

"Oh, it's you Vicar," said Fred Williamson, suddenly deflated, "We'd better swap information for the insurance."

A traffic warden wandered slowly up to them, the deliberation in his stride stoking the anticipation in his sadistic streak. His name was Adolf King, and Vincent knew this because he had recently baptised Adolf's daughter, Queenie. Adolf looked Fred in the eye from a distance of twelve inches.

"I think you ought to be aware, Sir, that, in a case where the back of a stationary car is driven into by a moving car, it is always — ALWAYS — the fault of the second driver. You, Sir, rammed the vicar's stationary car, and the blame lies with you."

"He slammed his brakes on with no reason, there was nothing I could do," blustered Fred.

"He slammed, but you rammed," retorted Adolf, now really enjoying himself, "and I'm a witness."

Vincent, still shocked, but feeling suddenly delivered by his unexpected ally, blurted out in surprise a verse from his Bible reading for the day, Isaiah chapter 12 verse 2: "Jehovah is my strength and my song, and has become my salvation."

"In that case, Vicar," responded Adolf, "I'm a Jehovah's witness," and off he went, feeling enormously pleased with himself.

After Vincent had parked the car and got rid of Fred, he popped into the newsagents and purchased a copy of The Yawtown Gazette. There was a large picture of himself on the front page, taken at a recent garden party, and the headline read: Pensioners driven out by heartless vicar. The Ladies' Club had taken their story to 'The Big Yawn', and slightly embellished it. The reporter had done the rest. Vincent had a sick feeling in his stomach, and began to feel weak. He just managed to get to the car, sat for a few moments, breathing heavily, and then resumed his drive to Eastern General. As he went, he became aware that the prang had holed his silencer, and the engine noise kept roaring into double forte. Vincent fancied it was shouting out, "*Brrm brrm, heartless vicar, brrm brrm, heartless vicar,*" and that everyone was looking at him and saying, "*Oh look, there goes that heartless vicar,*" so he put on his spectacles and flat cap and sank his neck into his coat.

At the hospital, Janet was waiting for him. She had seen the paper and was full of fight. "You'll have to get your side of the story over and put the record straight," she counselled. "These occultists were bound to have a go what with all the progress we've been making. See if you can get yourself on Radio Yawshire and give them what for."

Vincent didn't really think he was capable of doing that, but neither did he feel like saying no to Janet.

As Vincent opened the vicarage door and helped Janet in, the phone was ringing. He rushed to the study and it stopped as he touched the receiver. Vincent went to the toilet. As he got there, the phone rang again. Vincent returned to the phone again. It stopped just before he picked up the receiver. He tried the toilet again. He was just washing his hands when the phone went again. This time he ran with wet hands and triumphantly said, "St Agatha's Vicarage," down the mouth piece. As his wet hand squeezed harder on the receiver, it shot out of his grasp and crashed on to the desk. Vincent picked it up again and said, "I'm so sorry, is there anybody there?"

"BBC Radio Four's *The World Today* programme here. We're running the story about the poor ladies you've drummed out of your church and would like to give you the chance to put your point of view. It would be a live interview in a few minutes time."

"Live interview? "

"Do it," hissed Janet, who was listening at the study door.

"What will the questions be?" asked Vincent.

"Just, 'Could you tell us the story from your point of view?'" replied the voice. Vincent thought he could do that, so he said yes.

Moments later Vincent heard the familiar voice of the star interviewer, Peter Paxo. "Hello Mr Popplethwaite." Vincent froze in terror.

"Hello, is there anybody there?" shouted Paxo.

"Yes, hello, I can hear you Mr... er... Stuffing" replied Vincent.

"Are you proud of kicking these poor ladies out of your church and stopping their harmless fun, Vicar?" sneered Paxo.

"Well er... er... actually this group... er... er... hired our hall but broke our rules — they smoke in it, they bring their black cats in, and they play with a... er... er... what do you call it? er... 'weeji' board. And all we did was tell them to stop or they couldn't hire the hall any more. I don't really see what all the fuss is about. We've got some Christian standards and I don't see what's wrong with that."

"The point is," shouted Paxo, "you get precious few people in church these days, don't you, even before kicking some out. The church should accept anybody shouldn't it?"

"But they don't come to church, they only hire the hall. We've got more people coming to church at the moment. Don't write us off Mr... er... er... Sage, it's never over till the fat cat sings."

"Well it seems like the fat lady sang for the ladies' group. Thank you for talking with us Mr Thwopplepaite."

The sweat was pouring off Vincent and he was shaking all over. Janet was shaking as well. 'Mr Stuffing' she kept repeating. "'Mr Stuffing'! You were brilliant, I'm so proud of you," she eventually gasped before convulsing again.

The moment Vincent put the phone down, it was ringing. Suddenly, the whole country was after him. Local radio stations from Plymouth to Carlisle wanted to interview him. Two television stations wanted to come and film him. One offered to fly him by private jet to a television studio to take part in a discussion about religion and the supernatural. Three people rang to tell him what an evil vicar he was. One rang to tell him that the black cats would get him for this. And several others rang to congratulate him on his courageous stand and his brilliant 'Stuffing' joke. Eventually, an exhausted Vince staggered upstairs, the phone unplugged, to join Janet in bed.

As he was climbing in, the doorbell rang. Vince trod wearily downstairs and opened the front door. It was the leader of The Ladies' Group, come to give him a piece of her mind. She was carrying her black cat. Just as she was beginning to call him the names she had been rehearsing, Charger flew past Vincent and leapt at the cat. The cat shot out of the 'Lady's' arms and down the pavement, Charger in hot pursuit. The lady turned and chased Charger, issuing threats against him if he so much as touched Tabitha. However, Charger, being a golden retriever, was never in danger of getting close to his quarry and broke off the chase just near an enticing smell on the lamp post. But the lady continued chasing Tabitha until both were out of sight. Vincent enticed Charger in with a biscuit and then gave him a cold sausage as 'a thank you'. Saying a prayer of thanksgiving to the God who had delievered him from the hand of his enemies, Vincent laid his head on the pillow.

"They've got the black cats, but we've got the golden retrievers," said Janet, "We can't lose! If God and Charger be for us, who can be against us?" The bed shook as Janet giggled and convulsed.

As she did so, the doorbell rang again. Vincent wrapped his dressing gown round him and plodded downstairs. It was a delivery man with a box and a note. Vincent opened the box and was mystified to find twelve packets of Paxo Sage and Onion Stuffing. So he opened the envelope and read the note:

From a friend whose leg you buried,
to the strains of BCP,
To a sage who knows his onions,
And stuffed the BBC!

Chapter 11

◆

It was Lee's turn to take the confirmation group, for which Vincent was profoundly grateful after his stressful week. Lee had once again decided to use his counselling training from college, and enquired of everyone what was worrying them about the confirmation.

"I'm rather large and not as young as I was," confessed Mrs Finnigan, "and I'm worrying about whether I'll be able to stand up again when I've knelt in front of the Bishop."

"I shouldn't worry about that, it's biblical to be large you know," responded Lee brightly. "We know that from the woman of Samaria." Mrs Finnigan looked blank. "The woman of 'Some Area'", repeated Lee, hugging himself in delight. Ruth's look could have shrivelled him, but, fortunately, he never noticed it.

"Well I was worrying because I'm so small I wonder if the Bishop's arms will be long enough to reach my head," joked Ron the verger.

"Oh, that's quite all right," said Lee, "there are lots of small people in the Bible."

"Such as?" grunted Ron, resigned to his fate.

"The third smallest man in the Bible," said Lee, warming to his task, "was Nehemiah — knee-high-miah — get it?! The second smallest man was one of Job's comforters, Bildad the Shuhite. And the smallest man was the Philippian jailor who slept on his watch."

"Could we start the confirmation group now?" asked Henry Forth wearily.

"Yes, we're talking about prayer tonight," said Lee, becoming businesslike. What do you think prayer is?"

"I have trouble with prayer," said Norris, because I can't do it. Not like you blokes can. You know, the professionals. You get up there in church and the fine phrases flow in the posh voice, and I can't do that. All I can do is say, 'Now then God, I'm in a mess as usual and I need thee to get thi finger out.'"

"That sounds like prayer to me," encouraged Lee. "The Holy Spirit is pictured in the Bible as the finger of God, you know, and he can do a lot with his finger."

"Like give you a good poke?" asked Mrs Forth, looking up from painting her nails, which she seemed to do constantly when not touching up her lipstick or tweaking her eye lashes. "I reckon he's given Henry a right good poke with his big finger recently."

"And what about you Bridget?" enquired Janet gently but pointedly, "What sort of a poke has he given you?"

"Well," said Bridget, blushing, "I think I've always believed. It's what I was brought up to. My parents were big Methodists. I did all my churchgoing by the time I was seventeen. Three times every Sunday including Sunday school. And I feel I'm coming home. And it seems real this time. Alive. I mean, just look at the change in Henry. Oh no, I don't suppose you can. You didn't know him when he had two legs did you?" she giggled.

"I can guess," said Janet briskly.

"Well, all I can say is, I've stuck by Henry Forth for thirty years through thick and thin, mainly thin, and said my prayers for him to grow up into a responsible human being, and it's finally happened. So I want to say thank you to

God and now I can be a visible Christian not a secret one, and it's a wonderful relief."

Janet and Bridget emerged from their conversation to find Lee doubled up in some sort of pain.

"I'm sorry Mrs Forth," gasped the trainee pastor, "I didn't know your name was Bridget. That explains why you've never finished painting your make-up!" Lee doubled up again while the rest looked on mystified.

"I'm sorry you find it funny, young man, but my parents were called 'Waters' and there were no jokes then. I've got Henry to blame for that as well as most things."

Janet was on the point of dragging Lee out by his ear and telling him to grow up when Peter said, "What I don't understand is that Jesus said, 'If you ask anything in my name I will do it', but it's not as simple as that is it? If prayer like that really worked it would make life easy, wouldn't it? All our wishes would come true." For some reason, Peter had fixed his gaze on Vicki. "But Christians don't seem to have life especially easy. The reverse if anything. So what's going on? Does prayer work or doesn't it?"

"Well, Peter," Henry said condescendingly, assuming the mantle of elder statesmen to which he was entitled by age and no other qualification, "it's the 'In my name' bit isn't it? That hymn 'Forth in thy name I go', means Henry Forth living in Jesus' name not his own. Being his representative. Asking for what Jesus wants rather than what Henry Forth wants. It's like being a sales rep. I used to be a rep for Brylcreem. I toured the barbers in Brylcreem's name but it didn't mean I got a free hair cut did it?!"

"What's Brylcreem?" asked Peter, puzzled.

"It's that grease they used to plaster on hair instead of washing it in the days before showers," explained Janet, remembering.

"In the days before indoor plumbing more like," muttered Bridget.

The door opened, and Vincent shambled in with cream cake for all.

"Right, here we are, it's costing us a fortune in cream cakes at the moment. I hope you're all putting at least three cream cakes in the collection plate each Sunday!" he said. Once, Vincent had had a sense of fun and humour, but that had been squeezed out of him by decades of offences taken, of defeats born and expectations disappointed. Now that his ministry suddenly and unexpectedly seemed to be bearing fruit, the frozen joy at the centre of his Christian being was beginning to seep out. Lee seized on the biggest cake, and passed the tiddlers around. The phone rang. Vincent murmured, "His Master's Voice," and retired to the study in obedience. Janet, realising Vincent was making jokes like he used to, shed a tear from one eye. However, she kept her other eye firmly on Lee.

It was Mrs Brown on the phone. She lived adjacent to St Agatha's and kept a not altogether welcome eye on the place. She kept her other eye on happenings in the High Street. Mrs Brown had better things to do with her life than go to church, but she still felt herself numbered among the shining ones on God's side — a public-spirited respectable citizen who had never harmed an animal in her life and who kept her garden immaculate. The plaque in Mrs Brown's garden, however, uttered its timeless pagan challenge to the adjacent church — "Nearer to God in a garden than anywhere else on earth." Some were Anglicans, some were Methodists, some were Shoppers, and Mrs Brown was a Gardener.

"You should come at once, Vicar. There's a fearful commotion. The lights are flashing on and off, and the organ's playing loudly and out of key. I think it's the hell's angels — they've broken in!"

Vincent collected Charger and drove the half mile to St Agatha's in trepidation. As they stepped on the pavement outside, the church lights were flashing on and off, the organ was playing every stop and note at once, and the bells started ringing drunkenly. Mr Brown was on the pavement in his dressing gown. Vincent was startled by its silky and expensive appearance and mentally added it to the list of little luxuries his modest stipend preserved him from.

"We've rung the police," confided Mr Brown in a grave and unnecessary whisper. "There must be some pretty desperate characters in there, Vicar, take care."

Vincent, with an insane courage born only of force of habit, walked up the drive with his bunch of keys, Charger slinking behind, and unlocked the door. The Browns and twenty-three other neighbours all stood on the pavement, fifty yards away, watching him.

"Thank goodness you've come," wept Mabel and three other ladies as they emerged and embraced him. "Can you let us in the church hall, we're desperate!"

Apparently, the quartet had stayed behind to rehearse an extra item after choir practice, and the choirmaster had locked them in by mistake. They had been flashing lights and making noises for two hours before Vincent rescued them. He let them in to the toilets and wandered back to the road, grinning, with Charger at his side. As he got there, a police van arrived with a huge and hungry alsatian in the back. The officer collected the fearsome beast and said to Vincent, or, rather, his dog collar, "Hello Sir, what seems to be the trouble?"

"It's a false alarm, officer, some choir ladies got locked in, that's all."

"OK, Sir, there are ten patrol cars following me, I'll radio through to call them off." As the officer reached inside the car, the alsatian turned round and yawned hugely, showing off a large and impressive array of incisors. Taken by surprise, Charger whined loudly in terror and rolled over on his back in emergency submission. Startled by this and unnerved by the strange noise,

the alsatian leapt for security into the back of his van.

"Your dog must be a tough nut to outface Fang, Sir" smiled the policeman as he drove away.

Next morning, Vincent was standing on the pavement outside St Agatha's recounting the story of the locked in ladies and Fang to Frank. Charger lay on the pavement at his feet. Charger was getting very bored, and desperate to leap up and go for a run with Master. Even a walk through the graveyard would be something. But no, they just kept on talking.

"I've been thinking," said Frank, when he had stopped laughing, "perhaps we could put in a toilet at the back of church. We've got plenty of money from that legacy. And how about a re-freshment bar? Now we're getting full again on Sundays we could have two services, one for the 'straights' and one for the 'halleluias', and they could meet over coffee between the services. Or in the toilet!" he offered as an afterthought.

"Have you been talking to Janet?" quizzed Vincent, suspiciously. Frank looked blank.

"But we can't spend the money anyway. Cuthbert persuaded the PCC it was for a rainy day."

"It is raining," said Frank, "Showers of blessing after thirty years of drought. And anyway, you've forgotten — Cuthbert's 'reigny' day is over!"

"I don't know, it's a bit bold," dithered Vincent. "I've no more ever had the courage to do a building project and start a new service than Charger ever had to be a police dog and catch criminals."

At that moment, a man ran out of Marks & Spencers just down the road, carrying a rail full of top of the range clothes. He headed at high speed for the graveyard. Shop assistants in high heels were giving half-hearted chase. Charger looked up and came to life. At last, someone prepared to go for a run with him. About time too! He barked with excitement and ran after the man. Vincent and Frank ran after them, trying to retrieve Charger. Chasing down into the new part of the graveyard, Charger caught the man up and jumped up at him in excitement to give him his 'hello, I'm with you' lick. The man screamed, dropped the clothes, tripped on three pairs of trousers, and landed in a heap on Cuthbert Grimshaw's grave, shrouded in four denim jackets. Winded and defeated, the man eventually struggled to his feet and Frank, an inspector in the Special Constabulary, arrested him.

Vincent got the lead round Charger, not knowing whether to congratulate him or tell him off. But the shop assistants, rather than pick up their soiled goods, just wanted to cuddle their new hero. Charger by now was really enjoying himself, and Vincent basked in the reflected glory.

Janet's reaction to the story was predictable. "You've got to do it now Vincent Popplethwaite," she instructed. "Your bluff's been called. If Charger can catch criminals over Cuthbert Grimshaw's head, you can build toilets over it. Present it at the PCC tonight. Strike while the iron is hot."

"Yes dear," muttered Vincent, stoically.

Janet suddenly felt well enough to attend PCC that night, and she sat watching Vincent, expectantly, and maintaining eye contact. Frank whispered in Vincent's ear as the others wandered in, "I'll propose it if you don't."

Vincent was trapped. First, he recounted the story of the locked-in ladies, and then of Charger's triumph. Then he made the point that the church was getting very full again on a Sunday morning. "And I'm weary of all those complaints that either the service was too modern or it was too traditional. It would be nice to think we could worship God without complaining all the time. So I propose that we have two services every Sunday morning, one modern and one traditional, and that we build a toilet and refreshment area at the back so that the congregations can go to refreshments when they need them, and mingle over the toilet."

"Coffee", corrected Frank.

"Not now Frank, we're in the middle of a PCC meeting," retorted Vincent.

"Won't that make us a divided church Vicar?" asked Maggie, concerned.

"I think we're getting divided as it is," said Vincent, "and if both main groups have a service they really relate to, the friction will go. We can maintain contact over coffee and midweek."

"Yes," added Frank, "and we can build unity around a shared common vision of what we're trying to do."

Fred Williamson thought two services was a wonderful idea. "Let's get these 'happy clappies' off our backs and give us space to worship properly again. But we don't need a refreshment point. Sacrilege in a church that is. And if you're not pouring coffee into them, they don't need a toilet. If you want to be friendly, have a drink and go to the toilet you go to the pub not church."

"Thats always been *your* motto Fred," said Frank, "but what do the others think?"

Darren Clark was the token 'young person' on the PCC, and he didn't often speak, but he did now. "If you want young people to come to church you've got to have music they relate to. And you won't get people today by not being friendly. They want church to be a community because they haven't got it elsewhere anymore. I read that in my A level sociology book. And I think it's immoral the church having all this money when people are starving. I think it's a brill idea, and we should give any money left over from the legacy to Africa."

Fred growled and gave out heavy disapproval signals, but the discussion went Vincent's way from that moment, and the PCC voted by twelve to five to draw up a detailed proposal for the next meeting. Vincent managed to be pleased and apprehensive at the same time.

"It's going to be a busy weekend," announced Vincent during 'Any Other Business'. We've got a backlog of baptisms, and Lee is doing four on Sunday afternoon. Then we'vegottheconfirmation in the evening with a record number of candidates — I think it was twenty-four at the last count. I'm doing the rehearsal tomorrow night. The church will be packed and we'll need to bring some chairs up from the hall."

Janet went home on a high and hugged Vincent and told him he was wonderful.

"It's not me is it?" replied Vincent. "I feel like it's all out of control. God seems to be doing his own thing and arranging everything. It's most irregular in the C of E and only some of me likes it."

"That's the bit that's wonderful!" laughed Janet as she collapsed, exhausted, on the settee.

Chapter 12

◆

Next evening, it was Vincent's turn to be exhausted. His mixed bunch of candidates were not the easiest people in the world to organise. He had great difficulty with The One-Legged Club when it came to the matter of kneeling in front of the Bishop. But the biggest embarrassment was when he asked the group to check the confirmation register. Vincent had meant to write "Forth, Bridget".

"You've missed the 't' off the end of my name," said Mrs Forth, icily. It was nearly as bad later on when Vincent asked for favourite hymns that could be sung in the service and Henry asked for "*Bridge over troubled Waters*".

The phone was ringing as he returned home, so he dived into the study and picked up the receiver.

"Hello Vincent, it's the Bishop here. I'm sorry to say I've got the flu and can't be with you on Sunday. But it's alright, I've asked my new suffragan to step in for me, the new Bishop of Batley. He's a namesake of yours - Bultmann Popplethwaite. He's very lively, I think you'll like him."

"Oh, righ..., er... thank you Bishop," was all Vincent could manage.

For the next few days, Vincent lived in a state of dread. He didn't dare to ring round the confirmation group to tell them, and he agonised about whether he would be able to say the right thing to Bishop Bultmann. Even worse, the Bishop rang Janet when Vincent was out and she invited him to tea. Vincent suspected she had set up an interrogation.

Sunday morning passed off reasonably peacefully, and while Vincent took his survival snooze, Lee did the extra baptisms. It was all a bit of rush after lunch, and the church was full of people as Lee arrived. Some of them looked a bit miffed at being kept waiting, and three babies were crying already. Lee ran into the vestry, got changed in record time, and began the service. He was just getting the families nicely settled round the font for the actual baptisms, when he looked into the font and saw to his horror that he had forgotten the water. The font was as dry as the Kalahari Desert in a drought. Lee stood stunned for a moment, had a brainwave, composed his features, looked up and solemnly announced, "Please stand for the ceremony of the procession of the water." The crowd all stood as Lee walked with maximum dignity to the vestry. He closed the door behind him, scrabbled around desperately for the baptism bowl that fitted inside the leaky old font, put it under the tap, ran to the door, and then solemnly processed back to the font. The babies stopped crying as everyone

seemed extra-awed by the extraordinary procedure.

Afterwards, a large, loud man came up to Lee as he was carrying the bowl back to the vestry, and said, "You can't just throw that away can you? It's holy water now isn't it? What do you do with it?"

"It's the duty," said Lee, attempting maximum *gravitas*, "of one of the godfathers to drink the baptismal water."

The man grabbed the bowl and downed the lot before Lee could say another word. He just got to the vestry in one piece before collapsing in hysterics. On the way home, Lee called in on Janet in the hope of a cream cake but he was told firmly they were for the Bishop not a curate today.

"How did the baptisms go?" asked Janet.

"Fine, very smoothly," replied Lee in an offhand way.

At 4.30 the doorbell rang again and Vincent ushered the new Bishop into Janet's presence in the lounge. The small talk only lasted three minutes, and was mainly about the surname, when Janet realised Vincent's worst fears.

"Yes, we got a letter by mistake recently that was meant for you from a group called 'Unmask', asking you to 'come out'," she said levelly, looking Bultmann in the eye.

"Did you really?" said Bultmann in surprise. "I got it eventually. I'm sorry they troubled you as well. I soon sent them packing of course. After all, we've got seven kids at home and my wife vouches that they're all mine! It all came from an article I wrote about hating the sin but loving the sinner. *The Guardian* got hold of it and did a headline: NEW BISHOP SAYS "I LOVE GAYS". Actually, the first edition said: "I LOVE GAZE" , but they corrected it in later editions to "I LOVE GREYS". But they meant 'gays'. At least I think they did. Anyway, I'm no more gay than you are Chinese, not that I'm anti-gay, I'm just not one of them. They picked the wrong chap."

"Oh, that is good news," smiled Janet, "do have a cream cake. But could I ask you about '*The Bible as Pamphlet*'? Some of our confirmation group have read it and don't really agree with it."

Vincent tried to disappear under a cushion on the settee, but couldn't quite manage it.

"Oh, that old thing," replied Bultmann, with a twinkle in his eye. "I wrote that in my deconstructionist phase. It's amazing what a young man can throw out if he puts his mind to it. But I've grown up since then. Recently, I've been re-dating the Gospels, and do you know, I'm convinced they were all written before AD 70. So they're all authentic. Plodder & Strawman are publishing my new one next week. It's called, '*The Bible's a Big Book After All*'. I'll send you a copy."

"Do please have some more cream cake Bishop," gushed a beaming Janet. Between mighty munches Bultmann said, "Tell me Vincent, has the 'Brisbane Blessing' reached Yawtown yet?" Vincent had never heard of the Brisbane Blessing so he thought it probably hadn't.

"It's also known as the 'Reykjavik Recuperation'," prompted the Bishop.

Vincent had heard of that. "Oh that, yes I've heard of that. It's got as far as St Mark's, but I didn't think it applied to ordinary Anglican churches," he answered, reasonably. "Brother," said Bultmann, looking Vincent solemnly in both eyes, "Even Anglicans need recuperation. When I went on my pre-consecration retreat I went to the hot springs in Iceland to get away from it all and to pray for help like I've never prayed before. On the Sunday I went to Reykjavik Reformed Church and the minister there prayed for me and the Holy Spirit came on me in power. I spent three hours flat out on the floor of the church. The cleaner found me mid-afternoon. So I'm recuperated now and I've got the Spirit like I've never had him before. We all need recuperation, Vincent, if revival's to come," he ended fervently.

"Would you like the last cream cake Bishop?" enthused an excited Janet. Vincent looked horrified, as though he needed recuperation like a hole in the head.

However, fêted by Janet and fortified by cream cake, Bultmann arrived at St Agatha's for his first confirmation in a state of high expectation. He preached on the passage in John chapter 20 where Jesus breathes on the disciples and says, "Receive the Holy Spirit."

"They didn't just receive the Spirit theoretically," he said, theatrically, "but for real. It was obvious they had received the Spirit from the effect it had on them. Some of them spoke in tongues, they prophesied, they healed people, cowards became courageous, and the inconsequential changed the world. And today, it should be obvious when people receive the Holy Spirit.

You may have heard of the Reykjavik Recuperation, or the Brisbane Blessing." Three hundred mostly blank faces stared at the Bishop. "Thousands of Christians are collapsing under the power of the Spirit and waking recuperated and refreshed for service. I haven't been the same man since I went to Reykjavik."

"Bloody obvious that," muttered Fred Williamson from near the back.

Fortunately only the hundred and fifty-three people sitting closest to Fred heard him.

"And you," said Bultmann, pointing dramatically at the candidates, "I expect each of you to display clear evidence that you really have received the Holy Spirit. In a moment, I'm going to lay my hands on you heads and say, 'Confirm, oh Lord, your servant with your Holy Spirit.' Are you ready to be confirmed with the Spirit in reality as well as in theory?"

Vincent was quite happy for his people to be confirmed with the Holy Spirit for real, as long as nothing unusual happened. This seemed to him a proper Anglican compromise, for which he now fervently prayed.

The first in the long line of candidates to kneel in front of the Bishop was Simon, followed by Peter. It was the first confirmation he had ever done, and the Bishop had spent some time that day practising on his wife and memorising the words. He carefully spoke the words, "Confirm, oh Lord, your servant Simon with your Holy Spirit." Simon was then supposed to say "Amen", stand, bow, smile, and return to his place. Vincent had drilled him in this like a Sergeant-major. Simon didn't even say "Amen", let alone rise. He keeled over sideways and lay stretched out on the chancel steps like a boxer who had taken one too many on the chin.

Bultmann looked startled, but everyone else was aghast, especially Peter. It was with the most extreme reluctance that he took his place kneeling on the cushion in front of the Bishop. The Bishop repeated the words and Peter collapsed all over Simon.

As the candidates proceeded like recruits to the firing squad, Lee dumped the Bishop's mitre and staff he had been holding as his chaplain and went round to act as catcher for the candidates. He particularly enjoyed catching Ruth. Eventually, Henry Forth staggered up to the Bishop. He looked up at him and said aggressively, "I think you ought to know, Bishop, that I only have one leg, and knocking me over could have very serious consequences. Very serious indeed." Henry remained proudly standing, defiant. Bultmann put his hands on his head and said, "Confirm, oh Lord, your servant Henry with your Holy Spirit, but only a little."

"That'll do nicely thank you Bishop," responded Henry briskly. He turned and walked stiffly but triumphantly, picking his way through the bodies, back to his seat. .

During 'the peace' the candidates began to come round. As the offertory hymn was announced, the remainder were woken up by the treasurer, George Greenstall. George had been banking on a bumper collection to balance the month's accounts. Gradually the service got back to normal apart from a lingering bewilderment factor mingled with some awe and joy.

"It's wonderful," said Peter to Vicki, at the end of the service, "I've just done a hundred hour week and I feel like I've just had a week off. It's better than popping pills. Have I ever told you how beautiful your guardian angel looks?" Vicki stored that one up for her collection of unusual chat-up lines. Bultmann came round handing out advance copies of his new book to the candidates.

"It's alright, they came to me free because of the mistake on the front cover."

Peter looked at the cover carefully and read, "'The Bible is a Bit Book After All' by Bultmann Popplethwaite." Peter was bewildered and getting a little cross until Janet enlightened him and his face cleared

Vincent was still at the trembling and dithering stage, but was coming round as he noticed that all the candidates seemed well and happy again.

"You've got a Spirit-filled church here, Vincent, " said Bultmann, as he prepared to leave. "Well done!"

"Nothing to do with me," said Vincent gloomily. "It's all out of my control. I'm out of my depth."

"We all are brother," said Bultmann. "Go to Reykjavik," he urged, "find the blessing for yourself."

"I can't even spell it, let alone go to it on my stipend," smiled Vincent. I'll have to make do with the 'Batley Blessing'. Thank you for making the service so memorable."

As Vincent ushered the Bishop out, Henry Forth limped towards them. He had been scribbling during the final hymn and he presented the Bishop with his finished article. Bultmann read it, smiled, and promised a reply. He showed it to Vincent, who read:

One finger, one thumb, one hand on head,
One tap on the bonse and the Bishop he said,
"Fall over, fall over."
And they all fell over but one stood still,
Who'd shrivel the Bishop if looks could kill.
So now let choir and people sing,
In the kingdom of the blest,
The one-legged man is king!

Chapter 13

◆

A few days later, as Vincent opened the post over the marmalade, he discovered a letter from Bishop Bultmann. There was a nice 'thank you' note, and an enclosure to pass on to Henry Forth. Vincent remembered that Bultmann had promised Henry a reply to his doggerel. So, after a cup of supervised 'Fairdoos', he wandered over to the church where the Forths were part of an all day cleaning party. He found Henry hopping around the eagle trying to shine up the brass.

"I still can't get over all them bodies piled up around here," said Henry, pointing at his foot. "I reckon I got away very lightly. Very lightly indeed."

"I think the Bishop's replied to your dog... er... poem," said Vincent. Henry raised an eyebrow, opened the note, gawped at the episcopal lines, and froze as one receiving terminally bad news. Vincent, concerned, put his hands in a pastoral, comforting way on Henry's shoulders. Some sort of strange heat or electricity seemed to flow from his fingers. Henry crumpled instantly like a house of cards and lay at Vincent's feet, grinning strangely.

Vincent stared blankly at Henry and felt his hands, which had begun to hurt as though they had been burnt. Frank wandered over from the hymn-book trolley, picked up the poem and read it out loud:

The only king is Jesus, and he wants
to bless us all.
Recuperating frees us from the curse
of Adam's fall,
We shine and fly like eagles in the roof
of Heaven's hall.
But if you belittle by asking a little, you stop
the Spirit's fun,
The curse remains, my son, and you will hop
while others run.

"One or two mixed metaphors in that," commented Frank. "Hardly catterel let alone doggerel, but it seems to have done for Henry. I suggest we put a pillow under his head and leave him to sleep it off while we carry on."

"Interesting, that bit about the Spirit's fun," said Norris Grace, "I'd always thought God was a serious-minded sort of bloke."

"Nobody serious-minded would 'ave made my Henry," said Bridget, shoving a cushion under his head.

Henry Forth slept like a baby all morning as the others worked around him. Eventually, Frank started taking orders for lunch. Chip butties seemed the order of the day. Mabel, who was too inhibited to eat chip butties, said, "A small cod for me please Frank."

"Me too," said a voice from the floorboards, "That'll make five loaves and two small fish. That's usually enough to go round."

"Welcome back Henry," said Frank. "How do you feel?"

"Recuperated," said Henry, as he struggled to his feet. "That vicar packs a powerful punch. Do you know, my new leg seems to fit a lot better all of a sudden." Henry started to walk around the church in a normal sort of way for the very first time. He grinned, then he laughed, then he jumped, then he tried to run. Then he nearly fell over, and everybody laughed.

Frank and Lee blinked in the sunshine as they emerged from the church gloom. Turning left into the High Street, they strode briskly past 'Gardeners World' in the direction of 'The Fish Plaice'. A lady was putting out the garden centre wheelie bins. Frank recognised her as a regular and reliable member of the 8 a.m. communion service for which she was sidesman every time there was a fifth Sunday in the month. Her name was Agnes Day. Lee had been waiting some time for this moment.

"Behold the lamb of God that taketh away the bins of the world," he declaimed.

"Yer what?" asked Agnes, scowling.

"Ignore him," counselled Frank, as he frog-marched Lee into the chippie. "I'll see you soon at communion, Agnes," he called out.

"Nine weeks on Sunday, Frank," shouted the regular member.

"You've got to learn there's a time and a *plaice* for everything," hissed Frank. "Now *plaice* the order and stop playing life for laughs!"

"I've come for the church working party order," said Lee brightly, over the counter. "It's five chip butties, two small cod, and the vicar will do the rest."

"I might as well be honest with you," said Henry, between mouthfuls of small cod, "I was very dubious about that place the Bishop went to. It sounded a dangerous place for our vicar. What was it called now? Ah yes, 'Wreck yer Vic'—wasn't it? But I think it must be a marvellous place now. Where is it? I could take the wife in January. Is it in the 'Winter Sun' brochure?"

As they finished lunch, a middle-aged man in thick glasses and a business suit walked quietly in, yawned, and said hello to Vincent.

"This is Mr Duckworth, the architect," announced Vincent. "I've asked him to have a think about our plans." Mr Duckworth had been coming to St Agatha's as its architect for longer than anyone could remember, and had never been comissioned to do anything more exciting than a repairs list every five years. Cuthbert Grimshaw had seen to that. It was so far down his list of priorities that it usually took Mr Duckworth about the five years to write the list. Mr Duckworth's contempt for St Agatha's lack of imagination was matched only by St Agatha's contempt for Mr Duckworth's lack of urgency.

"Plans?" said Mr Duckworth. "Did you say 'plans'? That'll be a first. No one's ever had 'plans' here before. What sort of plans?"

"We'd like to install a toilet at the back of church, and a refreshment bar," stuttered Vincent, hardly believing he was saying this. "And we want to create a space at the front for a worship group at a new modern service we're planning. And we wondered about extending the balcony for a crèche area." He added this one on instructions from Janet, who had thought of it yesterday evening. Mr Duckworth stared at him.

"Toilet? Refreshment bar? Worship space? Crèche facility? Does Mr Grimshaw know about this? "

"I doubt it," said Vincent, confidently.

"Isn't he churchwarden anymore then?" enquired the architect.

"No — I am," said Frank.

"Has he moved house then?" asked Mr Duckworth, still unsure of his ground and afraid of his erstwhile tormentor.

"Yes, in a manner of speaking," replied Frank. "He doesn't live in Azalea Gardens anymore, he's come to live in the graveyard here instead."

Mr Duckworth stared at Frank for a while as this news filtered through first to his brain and then to his tongue.

"Right," he said, timidly at first. Then he repeated it with a little more confidence. "Right!" Finally, he managed it decisively, "Right!! I'll go and get the tape measure."

It was a different Mr Duckworth who returned with his tape measure and clipboard. A Mr Duckworth no one at St Agatha's had ever seen before. He had come alive. He talked twice as fast as he ever had before. He gesticulated. He exuded enthusiasm. Best of all, he had ideas. Until today, Vincent had had no idea that Mr Duckworth had ideas. But soon he was teeming with them. Suddenly, his face clouded and he stopped. "Of course, this'll cost a pretty penny, how much money have you got?" he enquired.

"We've had a big legacy, and we'll have a gift day if necessary," replied Frank. "Just keep those ideas coming!"

When Mr Duckworth left, he promised to go straight back to his drawing board and produce some plans by next week. "We could have this done within nine months," he announced. "I must dash now, I've got work to do!"

As Frank and Vincent sat and grinned at each other, Henry came back in from the graveyard, where he had been doing some tidying. "Come and look at what I've found everyone, it's a goodun!" They all trooped after Henry to the oldest corner of the graveyard. Henry had been cleaning up a tombstone and uncovered some faded writing. It seemed to be a poem.

"I think I've cracked it," said Henry, and read:

Remember me as you pass by,
As you are now so once was I.
As I am now so you will be,
Prepare yourself to follow me.

"Good poem, that, isn't it?" said Henry.

"It's up to your standard of dogg ... er... poetry is that," said Vincent. "He must be one of your ancestors! Let's see if we can find a name."

They scratched away some more mould and muck and up came the poet's name: Henry Furze, 1793.

"It is!" shouted Henry. "Henry the Furzt — it's my ancestor! And I am prepared to follow him, what's left of me, thanks to you Vicar, God bless you!"

Vincent wandered back home after a satisfying day's working party with his heart full of the joys of parish ministry. For the first time in many years he was vicar of a happy and growing church. God had stirred himself and people's lives were changing for the better. He looked forward to telling Janet the Bishop's poem. She was in a lot of pain from her joints, but for the first time ever, she had a team of praying people behind her. They seemed equally faithful at praying spiritual life back into the church and at knocking back cream cakes. And now the church was going to be re-ordered and a new congregation started.

It was heady stuff for a plodder, and he gave his thanks to his Lord as he walked. *But why now Lord, what's it all based on now?*

"Like I said before," came the familiar and slightly exasperated voice in his head, "just the usuals."

Oh, you mean the prayers of the people and the suffering of the saints, said Vincent, remembering.

"I mean the prayers of the people, the suffering of the saints... and the blood of the martyrs," said the voice, suddenly turning gentle.

Vincent felt as though he had been stabbed. *But why can't we win without martyrs and suffering like all those recuperating charismatics seem to?* asked Vincent, pathetically.

"They'll learn," said the voice. "'Happy Clappy' is kids' stuff; self sacrifice is for grown-ups. If you won't bear a cross you won't wear a crown. You only get close to me when you feel the nails. So don't be afraid of them."

Vincent told himself it was just thoughts inside his head, but he didn't believe himself. He told himself that martyrs didn't happen any more in the C of E, but he didn't believe himself. He told himself to shake it off and sing a hymn tune, but he couldn't obey himself. In awe and dread he opened the vicarage door.

Chapter 14

◆

To his immense relief, Janet beamed at him from the settee.

"Hello my love, I've been waiting for you," she said. "We had a wonderful 'prayer and cream cake' meeting. Maggie's going to have one at her house next time. I think I've got them well and truly launched now. It was all a bit much for me, I'm afraid, but it was worth it. I prayed again after they went, and I've seen the Promised Land!" Vincent looked puzzled. "The new St Agatha's — I could see it in my mind's eye. It'll be wonderful. Did you talk to Duckworth about it?"

"Oh yes, he got quite excited. He'll send me a first plan next week. He arrived a tortoise and left a hare. It was amazing!"

"It'll be something to occupy you," said Janet, mysteriously. Something seemed to shift inside Janet's head, and she shuddered.

"Vince, I've heard the singing, and I can't wait to join the choir. Hold my hand," she muttered. As Vincent reached out, Janet convulsed again and fell on to the floor, unconscious. Vincent screamed at the top of his voice, "NO," then ran for the phone. He put a cushion under Janet's head, cradled her gently, and wept tears of anguish onto her unseeing face.

"Oh, it's you again, Sir," said the ambulance-man. "Where is the lady?" Vincent, unable to speak, took them into the lounge. With an oxygen mask over her face, Janet was soon speeding to Eastern General, with a shocked and shaking Vincent trying to avoid getting in the ambulance-man's way as he worked on her while his colleague cut his way through the rush hour traffic.

They put Janet in a side room at the hospital. Ruth came in and gave Vincent a tearful hug. Peter examined Janet carefully, and sent her off for X-rays. "I'm afraid Janet has had a very serious stroke this time," he warned. Vincent's throat was so constricted, he found it hard to breathe, let alone swallow. His stomach was knotted up, and his fingers and toes clenched up.

He sat by the bed and shook. Was this a nightmare? Could he wake himself up from it? Janet returned from X-ray, still unconscious, and Ruth made her comfortable. Vincent sat and held her hand.

"Do you see that?" asked Peter, in awe and wonder. "There's an army of them. They're blinding me!"

Vincent was beginning to wish either Peter would keep his angels to himself or that God would let him see them too, when Janet began to mutter. He strained to catch what she was saying. Suddenly the voice cleared and she said simply, "Andrew!"

"Who's Andrew?" asked Ruth, gently.

Vincent just sobbed and couldn't speak. After a while, Janet squeezed his hand and this seemed to give him the strength to regain control.

"Andrew was our son. He lived for an hour. No one around here knows about him. We never had any other children." Vincent sobbed the secret tragedy of his life out in great hot tears that landed on his dying wife's cold hand.

"The hand," he said at length, "it's beautiful again." And indeed it was. The twisting of the arthritis had vanished and the hand seemed released from its bondage.

"Hello Andrew," whispered Janet, and her contorted face unravelled in the most beatific of smiles. Vincent followed the direction of Janet's eyes and scrutinised the air, but he could see nothing.

"Hello Andrew," smiled Peter.

The sun came out from behind a black cloud and streamed directly through the window. There were four panes in the window frame and the central dividers cast the shadow of a cross, which landed perfectly on Janet as she lay on the bed. For some time, Vincent watched Janet, transfixed, as it were, on her cross. Her beauty seemed to him to return to face and body. Eventually he mumbled:

> In the old rugged cross,
> stained with blood so divine,
> A wondrous beauty I see.

And Janet whispered a reply:

> I will cling to the old rugged cross
> And exchange it *this* day for a crown.

"That fat one looks like it's singing, but I can't hear anything," said Peter, peering into mid-air at his angels.

"I can, it's beautiful, it's magnetic, it makes me want to go with it," said Ruth quietly.

In a hoarse whisper from the back of her throat with her final breath, Janet said,"It's over." She squeezed Vincent's hand for the last time, and was gone. The sun went behind a cloud and the cross disappeared. Peter saw and Ruth heard nothing further. They slipped out of the door as Vincent hugged Janet for the last time and whispered tender, secret things to the strength and light of his life.

At length, Vincent sat on the chair with head buried in shaking hands, sobbing painfully through his twisted up gullet, and saying, "Andrew, Andrew, Janet my love, Janet my love, Andrew," time and again. Ruth returned with a cup of tea, but Vincent could not be comforted. Eventually, exhaustion brought his tears to an end, and Peter was able to lead him gently out of the room. He guided Vincent to the hospital chapel.

"Thank you for the privilege of being with you," said Peter, as they sat in the chapel. "It was the most wonderful death. And you know for certain that Janet and Andrew are both in heaven. I'll leave you to pray for a moment."

Vincent looked up, and in front of him was a wall hanging with Jesus on the cross wearing a very visible crown of thorns. Around the cross were the words: "Be faithful unto death and I will give you the crown of life."

My love was faithful and has the crown, but I don't know about me, he croaked shakily to the wall hanging.

"He who calls you is faithful, and He will do it," said the voice in his head, quoting Thessalonians.

He'd better, because I can't, Vincent replied.

Ruth came in with Vicki, and this time Vincent managed a few sips of tea.

"I'm just going off duty, so I'll take you home now," said Vicki. Vincent mumbled thanks and Vicki took him to her car. Charger greeted him at the door, and demanded all the cuddles Vincent was capable of. Then Lee arrived, and hugged Vincent and told him what a wonderful person Janet had been. He promised to stay all evening, and to return tomorrow to answer the phone calls, which quickly became legion. For the first time in his life, Vincent was being cared for by others, instead of the other way round.

Sleep was denied Vincent that night. Sometimes he lay down and stared at the ceiling in disbelief and panic that Janet was no longer there beside him. Sometimes he sat and cried and felt ill. Sometimes he paced the floor, unable to prevent the inner stress propelling him into activity. The future was an unknown country he did not wish to visit. He had visited a newly-made widow or widower hundreds of times before, but only now did he experience for himself the enormity of emotion unleashed by the bereavment.

He wished he was dead. But most of all, he wished it was yesterday and Janet was still alive. He talked to God, he prayed to God, he shouted at God, he craved comfort from God, he demanded answers from God. He threatened God that he would never speak to him again.

Eventually, the voice seemed to respond: "Janet is with me now. She's come home. You can still be close to Janet if you stay close to me. But you can't be close to me if you don't feel the nails. Be faithful to me and you'll have strength for today and bright hope for tomorrow." Vincent didn't want to feel the nails, but eventually he capitulated to the voice and ceased his argument with the Almighty.

As he came to dress, something in him demanded a token effort to reach out for the normality that had been destroyed. He dressed in his clerical shirt as usual, and took Charger for an early morning stroll. He found he was afraid of meeting people. Either they wouldn't know and he would have to tell them, or they would know and no one would be able to think what to say. Having to tell someone would only comfirm the reality he would rather wake up from. To talk about Janet in the past tense when she was alive only hours ago would be more than he could bear. So Charger was quickly back home. As they arrived, Mabel was on the vicarage doorstep.

"Oh Vicar, I'm so sorry. Janet was my hero. Would you allow me to do some cleaning and shopping for you?"

"Not today, Mabel, maybe later, come in for a moment anyway."

"I had a *fiancé* once," said Mabel. "He was killed in a motor car accident. So I know a little bit how you feel. It's only God pulled me through. Even now, I find it hard to concentrate in sermons, I just think about Tony."

Vincent now understood a little bit more the mystery that was Mabel, but he quickly had enough of her and led her to the door.

"We'll all be praying for you, Vincent," she said as she dragged herself away choking back the tears.

The next few days seemed to Vincent so vivid yet so unreal. He increasingly had to accept this was a nightmare he was not waking up from. The Bishop had recovered from the flu, called on him and volunteered to do the funeral service. He made Vincent talk about Janet for the first time. He found it immensely painful but surprisingly helpful. So many people were praying for him that strength seemed to flow into him from the outside. He told the Bishop he would like to read the lesson at the service.

St Agatha's overflowed with humanity as Janet was brought in for the last time. As Vincent got up to read the lesson, he said, "Jesus tells us, 'Be faithful unto death and I will give you the crown of life.' Janet was so faithful in her prayers and her commitment that I think they hastened her death. I intend, with God's help, to be faithful to you and to Our Lord now that I am on my own. Please bear with me in my weakness and uphold me in your prayers." Vincent's face seemed to shine as he read with a new confidence and authority the whole of 1 Corinthians chapter 15, the great chapter about resurrection. He finished with the words:

> Where, O death, is your victory?
> Where, O death is your sting?

> ... But thanks be to God! He gives us the victory through our Lord Jesus Christ.
> Therefore, my dear brothers, stand firm. Let nothing move you. Always give yourselves fully to the work of the Lord, because you know that your labour in the Lord is not in vain.

The Bishop spoke about Janet's humour and faith and prayer life. But the main thing he wanted to say was that Janet had been at the heart of St Agatha's recent revival. In fact she had imperilled herself with her sarificial prayer life. "She is at the heart of what has happened here, and she will continue to be at the heart. Be like her. Be praying people. Use her as your example, and draw others to trust in Jesus, who is the way through death to heaven. And make sure you carry forward her vision of a re-ordered St Agatha's ready to take the gospel forward to the future."

Vincent's heart filled with pride in his Janet as he prayed that this would be her legacy. They sang,"Thine be the glory, risen conquering Son, endless is the victory thou o'er death hast won", as the last hymn. Even Mr Berry shed a single tear as Janet was laid to rest in a corner of the new graveyard as far away from Cuthbert as possible. For the first time in his life, he forgot to send a bill. He did not enjoy this, and never repeated the action, believing it to be the one big mistake in an otherwise unblemished business career. But sometimes a good death moves even those who make their living by them.

As the days moved into weeks, Vincent got back to work because he had no alternative, and because he had Janet's vision to bring to fruition. And he found the strength to do so flowing into him from his familiar friend, the suffering servant whose nails he had had the privilege of feeling. Others rallied round. Frank was a tower of strength. Mabel kept the vicarage from becoming a 'dog-and-widower' slum. Charger was as foolish as ever and gave Vincent the first smiles of his new life. Others brought new pains. Some, who had always been happy to smile and chat to the Vicar now crossed the road to avoid him. Vincent wondered why and, imagining the best, assumed it was because they didn't know what to say. Mrs Finnigan, whom Maggie had brought to the guest service and who had joined the ranks of the 'recuperated' at the confirmation, told Maggie that she could no longer believe in a God who had done that to the vicar's wife, and was never seen in church again. Several people asked him within the first three months, "Have you got over it yet?"

Others, however, seemed to grow in Christian stature, and the church became even fuller on a Sunday. Vincent noticed it was the new people, not the old stagers, who brought their friends. The day Mr Broadhead returned down the balcony steps because it was full upstairs and had to sit in a choir stall, finally decided Vincent to start the second service. Soon after that, the building work began.

Mr Duckworth had been true to his word, producing plans and drawings like mediums produce ectoplasm. The toilet, refreshment bar, and worship space could be built out of the legacy. But the extended balcony with enclosed crèche area needed extra money. The PCC became grave. Those with one pound a week covenants to the church began making prudent noises. George Greenstall the treasurer reminded PCC members of their responsibility for paying the financial quota to the diocese on time and in full. Men who habitually faced a difficult challenge from the size of their Sunday joint became wise about biting off more than they could chew. Fred Williamson gave his opinion with a minimum of words and a maximum of bile: "Babies, nappies and potties are for smelly nurseries not the house of God."

Finally, Frank Williamson could stand no more. Normally, Frank sat on the back row where he could keep an eye on the others, observe who voted which way, and speak to the backs of their heads. For the first time in his life he stood up and went to the front to address the meeting. It fell silent.

"Jesus said, 'Suffer the little children to come unto me'," started Frank. "We want to attract families with small children, not put them off. Did you know Kevin and Miranda are expecting twins? What are they going to do with their babies? Play catch the wig with Mr Broadhead? We have a vision that Janet had first, and the Bishop has told us to implement. But it's first and foremost a vision from God for our future. So are you going to serve God or money? Now is the time to choose. I propose we go ahead with the balcony crèche, have a gift day to finance it, and I'll give the first £1,000 tonight."

Maggie immediately seconded Frank, and the PCC voted twelve to six for the crèche area.

The gift day was the most extraordinary day ever in the life of St Agatha's. They needed £40,000. The soundproof plate glass enclosing the crèche area, and the speaker system into it, helped make it so expensive. The average Sunday collection was around £300. There had once been a gift day for an organ repair of £1,500. When George Greenstall announced the amount given at the end of the special service grown men groaned and pessimists shouted for joy.

"The special collection plus amounts already given totalled £39,950," he said, and shook his head in disbelief. "I've counted it four times, and I still don't believe it, but there it is!" Vincent's happiest moment since Janet's death came when he slipped a cheque for the remaining £50 to George at the end of the service.

The building work proceeded surprisingly smoothly. The main problem came when the most popular pew in the building disappeared one Thursday afternoon. It was the back one. The space was needed for a circulating area now that the toilet and refreshment area were being built. Three habitual back pew denizens walked out of the traditional service in protest and were never seen again. This hurt Vincent even more than these things usually did because of his tender emotional state. On the other hand, the church kept on becoming a happier place as more and more of its awkward squad left. There were fewer and fewer people left to put newcomers off, so they tended to stay.

On the Saturday before the opening service everyone was invited to look round. The original idea of a toilet had expanded into a ladies and a gents, complete with outer lobby and urinals. The builders had got behind hand and forgotten to put the 'ladies' and 'gents' signs on the doors in the last minute rush. Mabel and her friend Doris wandered into the gents. Frank, standing outside, smiled and waited. He was quickly rewarded with two satisfying screams.

"Frank, what funny low down wash-basins you've put in the gents," scolded Mabel, as Lee emerged after them, giggling.

The special guest at the opening service was Bishop Bultmann."I love babies," he said. "I've helped create seven of them, with a little help from my wife, and the church can't have enough of them. I have pleasure in declaring this crèche room open!" Bultmann pulled a string and unveiled a plaque, the nature of which Frank had kept from Vincent as a surprise. It simply said, 'The Andrew Room'. Vincent nearly collapsed with surprise and emotion and stayed in the Andrew Room most of the day with a full heart and a crowded memory. Henry Forth found him mid-afternoon when he popped in to check the heating for the eveningservice.

"Vincent," said Henry, "I obeyed the command to 'Go *Forth* and multiply', and we had four children. Two times two, you see. In fact, it was more than obedience. I quite enjoyed it, even though Bridget's not the prettiest thing on earth. But you and Janet have more children than me. I'm one of them. You'll be a popular man in heaven, you'll be, and so will your Andrew. All them kiddies that screamed their heads off in here will want to meet the great 'Andrew Room' when they get to heaven!"

The phone was ringing as Vincent got back to the vicarage in time for tea.

"Miranda's had the twins this lunch-time," said Kevin. "Andrew and Janet are doing fine!"

"Yes, I know," replied Vincent. "Oh, you mean the twins? Andrew and Janet? Thats wonderful, Kevin, thankyou."

"Yes, and they've both got lots of hair," said Kevin, "so they don't need to be afraid of Aunty Mabel!"

"I'll look forward to the baptisms," said Vincent as he put the phone down and went to make his cup of 'Fairdoos'.

Chapter 15

◆

In the months after Janet's death, Vincent still kept the coffee in the filing cabinet, but now it was filed between 'Electoral Roll' and 'Funerals'. He had grown to like 'Fairdoos'. The shape of the jar, the unsophisticated aroma, the muddy taste, and the pledge of fair trade for the poor, brought Janet vividly back to him. As he made it, he distilled her goodness back into this world as its steam carried his adoration to the next. He forgot that he preferred proper coffee. He ignored his craving for caffeine, which gradually subsided. 'Fairdoos' meant Janet, and he drank it with enthusiasm. 'Fairdoos' meant justice for the exploited and he became Janet's disciple. No sermon was complete without an advert for that silver blend of responsible consumerism which freed the exploited pickers from captivity to their starvation wages. The

Yucca plant began to thrive. The 'Fairdoos' manager came to preach, and described his recent visit to the plantations. Vincent was no longer simply a yearner after Janet's simple goodness. He became a supporter in his own right. Sales boomed. Consumption, however, was another matter. The rumour that Frank Williamson used his bulk purchases as fertiliser for his prize roses was never believed by Vincent, though never denied by Frank. Henry was more forthcoming. "That coffee, Vince, is wonderful stuff. It's my new secret ingredient! Thou should see my leeks!"

The new service thrived, and The Andrew Room was a busy place come Sunday. But the Vicarage was a desert of human companionship. As the church grew, so Vincent's resilience at home shrank. It was not too bad in the mornings when scatty Mabel came to clean and cook and chat, but the dog and the whisky bottle proved inadequate companions as a day's work ended. The curer of souls was a lonely and increasingly exhausted soul himself.

On Mondays, Vincent kept a Vestry Hour between 6.00 and 7.00. The newly engaged came to book their weddings, and the new parents their baptisms, except that they called them 'christenings'. After a busy Monday, Vincent had particular need of the whisky bottle, as his own dead wife and child brought a heaviness of personal grief to bear on the superficial happiness of betrothed teenagers and unmarried mums. When Vincent was young, wedding couples always gave different addresses, when he was middle aged they always seemed embarrassed when required to expose their cohabitation. Now they seemd as untroubled by this as they clearly expected the vicar to be. Fornication had become respectable, and a wedding merely the biggest party excuse in town. The idea of virginity before marriage had become as laughable as no singing practice before a concert.

As Vincent mused gloomily on this one Monday evening as winter gave way to spring, he did not realise that his mood on the matter was partly generated by the after-effects of Mabel's suet dumplings. "Give me a responsible, old fashioned couple, Lord," he prayed.

Just then, Lee burst into the vestry. "Hi Vince," he quipped in an artificial, overfriendly falsetto. "No other customers yet?"

"It's not your turn till next week, Lee. What are you doing here?" enquired Vincent, wearily.

"It's all a matter of hats," said Lee, mysteriously. Just then, a nurse in uniform ran through the door.

"Sorry I'm late, someone died as I was coming off shift, are we in time?" asked Ruth, anxiously.

"In time for what?" blinked a bemused Vincent. "I'm doing the bookings tonight, not Lee."

"We're all doing the booking tonight, Vince, Ruth and I want to book our wedding," explained Lee patiently. Vincent stared at them wide-eyed as they grinned back at him, holding hands.

"I popped the question last week when I went to see old Mrs Hargreaves in Eastern General. Ruth came to give her an enema and it seemed like the perfect moment."

"You asked her to marry you as she gave Mrs Hargreaves an enema?" gasped Vincent.

"That's right. And she said yes, so here we are."

"Actually," corrected Ruth, "He said, 'Will you marry me and have a white wedding at St Agatha's and is Mrs Hargreaves going to make it?' I could hardly say no, could I?!"

Vincent spluttered for a while. He wanted to be happy for them and even he had noticed they seemed fond of each other. But he couldn't understand why a fine girl like Ruth had fallen for a foolish boy like Lee, and he was steeling himself to call on Mrs Hargreaves to apologise. As though reading his thoughts, Ruth said, "Lee has been learning a huge amount from you, Vincent, and he'll make a wonderful vicar before long. He's promised to keep his sense of humour to himself in public. And I've learnt a lot from Janet and you as well. We'll make a good team."

"But do you want to be a vicar's wife?" asked Vincent, concerned.

"Oh no!" replied Ruth. "I'm not the housekeeper-hostess-women's-bright-hour type. I'd like to do an ordination course myself and be a vicar as well. Then we'd be a real team."

Vincent shook in shock and spluttered in surprise. He had never opposed the idea of women priests because he couldn't think of a good argument against them. But they still terrified him. Eventually, something seemed to click inside Vincent's mental processes, and he smiled. "God had quite a future in mind when he sent me to St Barnabas's didn't he? I think you will make a very good vicar, Ruth. Much more sensible than some. Now let's fill in the wedding form before you give me any more shocks. Lee, we'll start with your side of the form. What is your name?"

Lee was about to say something fatuous, but was shrivelled by a glance from Ruth. “Lee Green,” he said solemnly. Ruth smiled in satisfaction and the form filling began.

Next morning, Vincent walked round to Mrs Hargreave’s house to apologise. To his surprise, the door was opened by Amazing Grace.

“She’s holding court with the neighbours in the front room,” whispered Amazing. “She had a wonderful time in hospital and picked up no end of juicy gossip. She was ever so cross when they sent her home so soon. She’s called the neighbours together to tell the tale.”

Vincent listened quietly in the hallway as Mrs Hargreaves’s wobbly but shrill voice cut effortlessly through the cavity wall. “And then the curate came to see me. So nice of him. Such a handsome young man. And not stuffy like the vicar. He told me a joke about a Hindu holy man, a Jewish rabbi, and an American TV evangelist. I’d come to church if I knew he was preaching. Then guess what! One of the nurses came round to help me with something personal and he leaned over the bed and said, ‘Ruth, will you marry me and have a white wedding at St Agatha’s, and can Mrs Hargreaves make it?’ And she said yes! It was so romantic. Better than *Gone with the Wind.* They'll make a lovely old-fashioned couple. Just like it should be. And it was so nice of him to invite me to the wedding right in the middle of his proposal. The home help's taking me out tomorrow to get an outfit. What do you think of that?"

"For once, Mrs Hargreaves, I'm lost for words," said the familiar voice of Mildred Masham. Vincent's legs buckled. Big Mildred had vanished from sight after her walkout and Vincent had never gone looking for her. He began to retreat, walking backwards through the hall.

"I came to apologise for something, Amaz... er... er... amazing really, Grace, but I don't need to now," whispered the 'retreatant' as he shuffled quietly backwards down the garden path.

Chapter 16

◆

It was the first warm day of spring. In the old days, Janet had always told Vincent what to wear, and he had obeyed. Now, he always seemed slow to react to weather changes and was usually perfectly dressed for yesterday. Vincent was hot and bothered as he arrived home. The phone was ringing as he entered the door. Mabel picked it up. "St Agatha's Vicarage," she said. "Oh no, I see, he's just coming in, I'll tell him and he'll be with you in ten minutes, bye."

Vincent stopped taking his coat off.

"That was Mr Berry. Walt Watson's been taken ill and he's due to do the 11.30 at the crem. I said you'd nip down and do it. Did I say the right thing?"

"Walt should have given up doing funerals years ago when he passed seventy-five. He's always being taken ill," mused Vincent grimly. "Of course you said the right thing, thanks Mabel, I'll go straight away."

The string vest and the wool suit were doing their job with utmost efficiency as Vincent ran up the path to the crem. The mourners were just beginning to arrive. Without hesitation, Vincent put his cassock and surplice over his jacket as he picked up last minute details from Mr Berry's oldest retainer. The hearse arrived, and calmly Vincent met the family at the door as though he had spent days preparing for the moment. As he entered the chapel, he realised that the council were as good at putting on central heating for yesterday's weather as he was clothes. The chapel was swelteringly hot. He struggled manfully on.

As he got to the commital, Vincent began to feel unsteady. He fumbled a few of the final words and crumpled over the final 'Amen'. The mourners stood impassively, looking at him. Vincent tried to get himself down the central aisle to the back of the chapel but he couldn't rise. Slowly he crawled to the back as the mourners looked down on him respectfully. It dawned on Vincent that they thought this was all part of the ceremony. The humble priest makes his pious exit on all fours. Mr Berry met him at the back door.

"Now then, Vincent, you look proper poorly, we'd better take you to casualty in one of the vehicles."

The oldest retainer whispered that the vehicles were all needed for the next funeral, and it would cost him to hire an emergency replacement from the Co-op. Mr Berry remembered his mistake over Janet and said kindly, "You're right Albert, send for an ambulance, it's no more than the reverend deserves." Vincent fainted twice more before the ambulance arrived, and Eastern General kept him in overnight for observation.

"Oh Vincent," said Mabel as he arrived home next morning, "you've been overdoing it haven't you. What you need is some good rest and nursing. I've rung Lee and told him you'll be off work for a week, and he's told Frank. I've changed your bed and aired your room, and I'll pop in each afternoon as well as each morning to check you're okay. Your too precious to lose you know!" Vincent felt too weak to argue and gratefully accepted the cosseting. In fact, as the days went by he began to like it. Mabel was so genuine in her devotion to him, and so seemed to have grown in confidence and common sense as she sensed his acceptance of her ministrations, that he felt himself growing even fond of her. He liked having her around.

One evening, Frank came round to share a medicinal whisky. Vincent told his friend about the emptiness he felt without Janet.

"I know how you feel. I felt so lost and lonely after Whin died. Best thing I ever did, getting married again, even though it's hard to shake off the new mother-in-law."

"It's too early for me to think like that, Frank. Who could replace Janet?" said Vincent, sadly, as he took a large gulp of single malt.

"No one could — that's not the point," persisted Frank. "They'll never be another Janet, but that doesn't mean to say you have to be on your own for the rest of your life."

"Well," reflected Vincent after a while, "I won't be on my own tomorrow. First day back and I've got the 'Incontinental Retirement Home in the morning. I wonder what they'll do to me this time."

At 10 am sharp, Vincent was setting up his communion table when one of the ladies, sitting in a far corner, summoned him over. She grabbed his cassock and pulled his face close to hers. In a thick emerald accent she announced, "I'm a Catholic and I don't hold with your sort. I'll be saying my rosary while you're at it over there."

"That's fine, Mrs O'Flaherty," said a relieved Vincent.

"And so will Mary," she added. Mary said, "Isn't he lovely, the reverend, I'd like it please."

"No you won't, you sit still," commanded the rosary keeper. Mary sat still and Vincent returned to his communion table.

As he began the service, he became aware that a loud debate was gathering momentum in the corner. Both Mary and Mrs O'Flaherty were deaf and both were talking at once. In fact, very soon they were both shouting at once. Vincent gave up the unequal struggle and returned to the corner to ask them to be quiet. By the time he reached them, the pair were on their feet and pushing each other. He was just in time to deflect a right hook that would have felled Marciano.

"Now, now girls, that's enough of that. You sit down and do your rosary Mrs O'Flaherty, and you come and sit next to me, Mary." Mrs O'Flaherty sat and Mary followed Vincent like a besotted puppy.

"Isn't he lovely, the reverend," she told the congregation as she sat. When Vincent got back to the vicarage, he wandered into the kitchen, where Mabel was mopping the floor, and told her the story. As she began to laugh, so did he. When Mabel stopped, Vincent kept on going. For months he had hardly smiled or laughed, partly out of grief and partly out of his feeling of respect for Janet. It would, so it seemed to Vincent, have belittled her loss. But suddenly, a floodgate was breached and the laughter burst out of him in torrents.

"You havn't caught the 'Reykjavik Rejuvination' from Mrs O'Flaherty have you?" giggled Mabel, and Vincent was off again.

Afterwards, feeling that a great tightness had gone from his inside, Vincent wandered off to St Agatha's, still chuckling quietly. He sat in Janet's old pew and said, *So what are you doing now Lord?*

"Still building," came the instant reply.

What with now? asked a sobered Vincent, suspiciously.

"Most of the usuals — the prayers of the people, the suffering of the saints, the blood of the martyrs and, oh, yes," said the voice, as though looking for things on a list to tick off, "the joy of the Lord. Suffering and joy — they go together like Yorkshire pud and gravy you know!"

Well I could do with some more gravy on my Yorkshire pud, Lord, retorted Vincent, but the voice had gone.

Vincent sat for a while, reflecting, but his peace was shattered by the sound of pushchairs banging into the outer door and the noise of hungry babies yelling.

"Even church doors are too narrow for these flippin' twin buggies," said Miranda as she crashed in. Following her was another girl with a single pushchair.

"I'm so glad I caught you, Vince," Miranda greeted him, "I want you to meet Charlene, and this is Charley her baby."

"Hello Charlene," smiled Vincent. "He's lovely. He doesn't look like he's missed many dinners."

"Charley's a girl," said Charlene briskly.

"Charlene wants to talk to you," explained Miranda, "I'll take Janet, Andrew and Charley off for a minute."

"The thing is," said Charlene, "I had a terrible time having Charley. They tell me I could have died. And I've had terrible pain since. And my boyfriend left me. And through it all, I prayed to God for help, and every time I prayed I seemed to feel strength coming into me. And I promised him if I came through this I'd take more notice of him in the future. And I did. And then I met Miranda at the postnatal class. And she told me about Jesus. And she said to come and see you. I'd like to be a Christian like Miranda. If I'm allowed. If you'll have me, that is, being a single mum and all."

Charlene looked at Vincent with big brown eyes. Vincent responded with a gale of laughter. "Of course we'll have you, with great joy. Welcome to our club for forgiven sinners and joyful sufferers."

Charlene looked at Vincent suspiciously, but was soon smiling as he told Miranda about the 'Incontinental'. Henry had insisted on having a pile of evangelistic booklets on the new church bookstall, and Vincent spent some time taking Charlene through one as Miranda encased the babies in The Andrew Room.

As Vincent walked back home for lunch, he was walking on air. He thought about the joy among the angels of heaven over one sinner who repents, and he felt he was sharing in the party.

When he got home, there was a terrible burning smell in the kitchen.

"I'm so sorry, Vincent, " anguished Mabel, "I left the meat in the oven too long. I started reading one of your theology books and I fell asleep. The meat's useless I'm afraid. So I've done you a giant Yorkshire pudding, with lashings of gravy. Is that alright?"

Vincent roared with laughter, gave Mabel a kiss on the forehead, and said, "Perfect, Mabel, absolutely perfect. It's the Lord's burnt offering in the oven, the Lord's. I'll have as much gravy as you've got please!"

As the summer went by, Vincent continued to gain emotional strength and even began to enjoy life sometimes. His patches of blackness still came, but they steadily became less frequent and lengthy. The strength of his resurrection faith sustained him and inspired others. Those who used to mock him now respected him. Those who used to respect him now revered him. As he grew in confidence in the Good Shepherd who was taking him through the valley of the shadow of Janet's death, so he grew in stature and authority. His ministry had never been fruitful until the last year or two, but now his confidence was reclaiming its lost ground. The Lord was restoring the years the locusts had eaten, and he was loving it.

He even found himself enjoying Mabel's company. Mabel had never thought of herself as having any importance before. Over the many years since her fiancée had been killed, she had never sought or wanted to be closer than the fringe of anyone else's life. It was safer to hide on the edge. It was wiser to avoid exercising what brain she had for fear of letting her deep pain escape from the self-preservation of her structured shallowness. It was better to be absent-minded than bereavement-minded.

But, suddenly, Mabel found herself important to the living person she most admired: her vicar. She had stepped into the breach, cleaning and cooking for someone whose ministry was touching the hearts of many. She had a purpose in her Christian life and she mattered. She attempted to bring her brain out of retirement and engage Vincent in sensible conversations. Sometimes she even succeeded. Once or twice she even learned something from his theology books while he was out visiting. As her confidence grew, so did her faith. Her prayer life blossomed as she developed the discipline of praying for Vincent during the bus ride over to the vicarage.

Three times she missed her stop, and had to make a second attempt from the terminus. Once, she started praying so fervently again that she ended up where she started an hour after setting out. She thought she loved her vicar as a good and faithful servant, but her devotion began to run even deeper than that. Her greatest desire was for Vincent Popplethwaite's highest good. She was in love.

As summer gave way to autumn, Frank invited himself over for a medicinal whisky, producing at the door a peculiarly pungent island malt purchased on holiday. It tasted of salt and seaweed and Frank raved about it. When they were settled deep in their armchairs and their cups, Frank said, "How are you getting on with Mabel?" Vincent took another seaweed sniff and salty sip as he reflected, "I've got to know her a lot better. She's more sensible than I used to think. She even quoted Augustine at me the other day. Lord knows where she found him to read. I don't think I could have coped without her. The house would have been a shambles and I would have starved to death."

"Best thing I ever did, getting married again," repeated Frank as he left that night.

Next morning Vincent said casually, looking up from his sermon notes, "Are you doing anything later?" Mabel had an appointment at 1.35 with her hairdresser, and was having afternoon tea with Maggie.

"No, nothing," she said. Vincent essayed timidly, "How about a walk in Yawtown woods and a pub lunch?"

"Oh, that would be lovely. Yes I'd love to come," replied an excited and devoted devotee.

The walk and the pub lunch became a weekly routine, and Vincent quickly realised it became the high spot of his week,

As autumn gave way to winter, Lee was on duty one Monday evening at the vestry hour. As he lounged in the vestry waiting for customers, he flicked through the weddings file, working out how many days to his own. He was thrilled when he worked out it was less than before. Just then, his boss wandered in.

"Hi boss," said Lee.

The boss cringed.

"What are you doing here? It's my week on."

"I've come to book a wedding, Lee."

"No, it's definitely me on duty today. For once I checked before coming out."

The boss took a deep breath. "Mabel and I have come to help you book a wedding," he explained, carefully. Mabel wandered in behind Vincent, looking sheepish, but grinning.

"But I know how to book weddings," lamented Lee.

"Yes, but you need the couple with you, to sign, don't you?" persisted Vincent.

"Where are they then?" enquired Lee, looking vacantly around.

"Here!" smiled Vincent.

Lee pointed weakly at Vincent and then at Mabel, and finally gawped as the light dawned. "Right Vincent," he asked, recovering himself, "What's your name?"

"Vincent Popplethwaite," replied Vincent Popplethwaite solemnly.

As the form filling proceeded towards the end, Lee said, "And on what date would you like the wedding?"

"We thought after Christmas if the vicar has a space," replied Mabel.

"Oh, that's when we're getting married, the Saturday after Christmas," responded Lee brightly.

"Oh no!" exclaimed Vincent in agony. "I'd forgotten that. I've promised Lee and Ruth I'd do their wedding then. We can't possibly get married that week."

"Yes you can," said Lee. "How about a double wedding? You marry us and then I'll marry you."

Vincent was about to tell his curate to start being serious for once when Mabel said, "Oh that's a brilliant idea. It'll be a wonderful occasion, and no one will need to buy two wedding outfits." Lee, his hairy idea reinforced, said enthusiastically, "Yes, it's killing two birds with one stone."

"Marrying, perhaps," said Mabel, "that's all."

The news of the vicar's engagement created a sensation in Yawtown. It became really big news when the press got hold of the double wedding. They came to the parish hoping to sniff out scandal, and left disappointed with only a feel-good human interest story. This was not what the editors wanted, so the press began to leave them alone. Nevertheless, on the big day itself, Frank had some of his 'Specials' posted outside to keep reporters at bay.

The people packed into St Agatha's as though they were cramming into a Japanese commuter train. The organist started up, "Here come the *brides*", and the two couples walked joyfully down the aisle.

"Welcome to our weddings," said Vincent. "First of all I'm going to marry Ruth and Lee, then Lee's going to marry Mabel and myself."

"I thought I was marrying you and Lee was marrying Ruth," blurted out Mabel, confused. The best men ushered her to her reserved seat, and Vincent proceeded with the ceremony. He preached on the story of the wise and foolish builders. The wise man built his house on the rock and it withstood the storms of life. But the foolish man built on sand and his life came crashing down around him. "I've been battered by the storms of life and bereavment. But I stand before you with a full heart today because the foundation of my life is the death and resurrection of Jesus. Our church has been battered by the storms of conflict and disappointments. But it has full pews today because the foundation of our lives has become prayer and sacrifice for God's kingdom. So if life in marriage or in church blows wintry, don't despair – it's never over till the fat – err, err – Jesus comes again. Just dig those foundations in the solid rock of the Saviour and pray for better times."

Then Lee and Vincent went to the vestry, where Lee donned his cassock and surplice while Vincent took his off. The congregation started to sing, "Through all the changing scenes of life", and Lee started to giggle. But Vincent shed a quiet tear as he listened to the words from Psalm 34:

> Through all the changing scenes of life,
> In trouble and in joy,
> The praises of my God shall still
> My heart and tongue employ.
>
> O magnify the Lord with me,
> With me exalt his name;
> When in distress to him I called,
> He to my rescue came.
>
> O make but trial of his love:
> Experience will decide
> How blest are they, and only they,
> Who in his truth confide.

Out they went again, and this time Lee married Vincent and Mabel while managing to stay almost serious.

"How do you spell 'Popplethwaite'?" asked Mabel, peering at the registers at the signing. "I'll have to learn it now, won't I?"

The receptions were in the church hall. The relatives were having terrific difficulty working out who everyone else was. But all seemed to go well. Later, the tables were cleared, 'everyone else' was invited back, and the entertainments began. Frank had spent some time preparing these, and he felt he had tapped all the major talent in the church. His only mistake was allowing Lee to tell his joke about the Hindu holy man, the Jewish rabbi, and the American TV evangelist. It was all very excruciating until Mrs Hargreaves shouted out the punch-line just ahead of Lee and brought the house down.

As the last act on the programme walked off stage, triumphant, Vincent turned to Frank and quizzed, "It's all over then?" His old friend leaned across to him with a twinkle in his eye. "It's never over till the fat lady sings," he murmured.

"Whatever did happen to Mildred Masham?" smiled Vincent, wondering.

"After she left us," Frank replied, "she went on holiday and her car broke down just outside the 'Dance with the Spirit' convention show-ground. The suspension was absolutely smashed. Anyway, they invited her in and she got, I think the phrase is, 'slain in the Spirit'. She's been going to the ‘hot pentecostal’ church on Fire Street ever since.”

Vincent’s mouth gaped open wider than at the dentists. “They don’t let her dance do they?” he gasped.

“No, but she still sings,” laughed Frank, as a large shadow fell over the stage and the great bulk of Yawtown’s newest hot gospeller rolled into sight. With devastating conviction and megaphone diction, she proceeded to break the decibel barrier and Handel’s heart in a unique rendition of “I know that my Redeemer liveth”.

“So do I, love, so do I”, muttered the happy vicar of Yawtown.